RIPPED

MARS FITNESS
BOOK 1

LINDEN BELL

Cover Design: Cate Ashwood

Content Warning: grief and loss of a spouse, description of fatal car accident, description of homophobic family, cheating secondary characters. Happily ever after guaranteed.

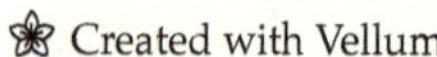 Created with Vellum

RIPPED

My life went from great to disaster in under five minutes.

CONNOR

It was just another Friday night, bringing home takeout for a cozy evening in with my boyfriend. Only to find him wearing nothing but a towel and my best friend frantically trying to put his clothes back on. It didn't take a genius to figure out what was going on.

Now I'm homeless and friendless and stumbling mindlessly through the doors of Mars Fitness, straight into Donnie's strong, comforting arms. He offers me a place to crash, then shows me how much more life can be when I have him by my side.

DONNIE

What was I supposed to do? Let the guy sleep on the street when I had a perfectly good guest room at home?

Letting Connor stay with me was supposed to be a temporary thing, but I never expected to feel so much around him. Attraction, joy, protectiveness—emotions I haven't felt in ages are suddenly breaking through my grief and overwhelming me.

It's been four years since my husband passed, and I've been caught in a limbo of merely existing ever since. But with Connor in my house and awakening all these feelings in me, maybe it's time I start living again.

Ripped is an age gap, nerd/jock, hurt/comfort MM romance between roommates who cuddle while watching classic movies. Expect steamy shower rooms, teary confessions, disapproving family, and brand new beginnings. It is the first book in the Mars Fitness series and can be read as a stand-alone.

CONTENTS

Chapter 1	1
Chapter 2	10
Chapter 3	19
Chapter 4	26
Chapter 5	32
Chapter 6	42
Chapter 7	50
Chapter 8	59
Chapter 9	67
Chapter 10	72
Chapter 11	79
Chapter 12	86
Chapter 13	93
Chapter 14	101
Chapter 15	110
Chapter 16	118
Chapter 17	126
Chapter 18	134
Chapter 19	143
Chapter 20	151
Chapter 21	157
Chapter 22	166
Chapter 23	173
Chapter 24	181
Chapter 25	188
Chapter 26	198
Chapter 27	207
Chapter 28	216
Chapter 29	222
Chapter 30	231
Chapter 31	242

Chapter 32   251
EPILOGUE   259

THANK YOU   265
ABOUT LINDEN BELL   267
ALSO BY LINDEN BELL   269

CHAPTER
ONE

CONNOR

Of the eight million people in the city of New York, I am the last person who should be in this room right now. Everyone is ripped, pumped, stacked, jacked, or however else you want to describe those guys whose muscles have muscles. Me—I'm a little chonky and I'd rather sit on the couch watching movies than work out any night of the week.

And yet, here I am, sweating my balls off in the back corner of a room filled with bikes, voluntarily getting shouted at by the hottest silver fox spin instructor in the city.

What am I doing here again? I ask myself that about twenty minutes into every spin class. It's partly because I've already paid for a year's membership to Mars Fitness, partly because exercise is supposedly good for me, and—okay, fine, partly because of sexy spin instructor Donnie.

"You can do it! Almost there!" His voice comes through the sound system, his soft British accent barely noticeable above the driving, frenetic music. Something fast-paced with a deep bass that booms through the walls, the floor, and me. The *thump-thump-thump* competes with the *whoosh-whoosh-whoosh* of my pulse until I'm one giant vibrating mass, hanging on to my bike for dear life.

"Five more! Four more! Three! Two! One!"

We all let out a collective groan of relief as the song finally ends and Donnie switches to something slower to cool us down. I drag a towel over my face with one hand and turn the resistance on the bike down to zero with the other. My feet spin uselessly in the pedals, my legs are jelly and I want to lie down on the floor and never get up again.

"Great job, guys!" Donnie's gaze sweeps across the room, pausing for a micro-second at every single person like he's congratulating us all individually.

When he gets to me, I can't help but smile back, feeling like I've gotten a gold star. This is part of why I torture myself too: that slightly delirious euphoria at the end of every class. I'm weightless, floating, and everything is bright and shiny and happy.

Donnie leads us through the cool down and the all-important stretches, reminding us to "hydrate, hydrate, hydrate!" The moment the song ends, half a dozen guys hop off their bikes, as if they've merely taken a leisurely ride through the park, and swarm Donnie. It happens every time. The gym bros are all ga-ga over Donnie, and hey, I don't blame them. He's hot. He's friendly. His accent is ear-candy. If I thought I had even a fraction of a chance with him, I'd probably be up there elbowing my way through.

But I don't, and besides, I've got a boyfriend waiting at home for me. A boyfriend who should've been at the class with me, who was the whole reason why I had a year's membership to one of the more expensive gyms in town in the first place.

Miles heard about Mars from some co-worker of his, about how it catered to gay men, how it was "the place to be." It was only after I let him strong-arm me into joining that I learned about the locker room—and the showers and the sauna and the steam room. There's a reason why Mars has branded condoms and single-serve packets of lube. They sit in giant fish bowls in every corner of the locker room. "Every good workout ends with a blowjob" might as well be the gym's tagline.

I strip out of my sopping wet clothes and dump them into my gym bag. There's already a steady soundtrack of muffled moans bouncing off the tiled walls when I get to the showers. I snag the last one and snap the privacy curtain closed. Even then, my dick plumps at the sound of guys getting off all around me. I give it a couple soapy tugs, then leave it alone. I don't need a hard-on while walking home and I'd rather come in Miles's ass than all over the floors of a public shower room.

After I change into my street clothes, I take a minute to scroll through the food delivery app for my favorite Mexican place. On the agenda tonight is tacos and binging the latest season of *Drag Race*.

CONNOR

Ordered dinner. On my way home!

Miles doesn't respond, but then, he never really does. He's got terrible text messaging etiquette.

"Hey, Connor! How was class tonight?" Sawyer, the guy who mans the front desk on evenings and weekends waves me down as I'm on my way out. He showed me and Miles around when we first joined and he always says hello when he sees me.

"Great! Donnie's always trying to put us in the grave."

"No shit." Sawyer laughs. "How's your boyfriend? What's his name? No, wait, don't tell me…" He scrunches up his face. "Miles?"

"Yeah, it's Miles."

"Where's his ass been? I never see him coming in with you."

Don't I know it. "He's not that big on the whole exercise thing."

Sawyer frowns at me. "What? Then why join a gym?"

Do I want to get into how Miles is always latching on to a brilliant idea, only to abandon it after a few months for the next shiny, new thing? I shrug at Sawyer. "Beats me."

"Well, tell your man to get his ass in here, okay?"

"I'll do my best!" I will do no such thing. I know a lost cause when I wake up next to it every morning.

Outside, winter is still clinging to the March air and the cold wind whips at my face. I pull my hood over my wet hair and hunker down for the walk home. Our apartment isn't too far from the gym. If my legs weren't little more than jelly, it'd only take me ten minutes. Right now, it'll probably take me fifteen.

I'm unlocking the front door of my building when a delivery guy rolls to a stop on his bicycle beside me. The light from his phone is shining on his face.

"You from El Pescador?" I ask him.

"Yeah, unit 3B?"

"That's me. Connor Hill."

He checks my name against the info he has, then hands over the heavy bag of food. I can already smell the delicious aromas of the tacos, and my mouth waters as I go inside. I'm starving. Miles had damn well be ready to eat when I get up there because I'm not about to wait for him to start.

The climb up to the third floor isn't fun on a normal day, but on spin days, it's murder. Not gonna lie, I have to stop a couple times to wait out the stinging in my muscles. By the time I make it up to the apartment Miles and I share, I'm *this close* to eating my tacos while collapsed on the floor.

"Babe!" I call out as the door swings shut behind me. "Food's here!"

There's a commotion in the bedroom like Miles is stumbling around and cursing under his breath.

"Babe, you okay in there?"

No response. In fact, it's gone silent. I'm about to poke my head into the bedroom to make sure he isn't dead when the bathroom door opens behind me. Wait, what? Isn't Miles in the bedroom?

"Oh, fuck."

I turn to find Miles standing in the bathroom doorway, wearing nothing but a towel and a look of shock.

"What's wrong?" I ask, even as my stomach starts to sink.

Miles's gaze flits over my shoulder and his eyes burgeon at what he sees.

"Hey, Connor."

The voice is familiar but there's something off about the way it sounds. I spin around. Wyatt, my best friend from film school, is standing in the bedroom doorway.

He's straightening his sweater like he's pulled it on in a hurry. His hair is standing up on end.

Was Wyatt supposed to come over today? I don't remember him mentioning anything.

On my left, Miles looks like he's about to have a panic attack. On my right, Wyatt looks like he wants the floor to open up and swallow him whole. My stomach is somewhere around my knees, but wait—don't jump to conclusions.

There could be a perfectly reasonable explanation for why they're acting so weird. This isn't the first time I've come home to find Wyatt at our place. He's never needed an invitation to drop by. We've all known each other long enough that Miles and Wyatt consider themselves friends and they hang out without me all the time when I'm busy.

Except their matching guilty faces look so fucking guilty.

"What's—" The rest of the sentence dies on my tongue. My stomach plummets out of my body. Miles and Wyatt exchange wide-eyed horrified stares that speak so many volumes, they're practically shouting.

I think I laugh. My precious tacos definitely go *splat* on the floor. Disbelief roars in my ears and I barely hear one of them say, "Connor, we can explain. Connor, wait!"

I'm already halfway out the door. Maybe if I run backward fast enough, I can rewind the last five minutes and pretend I didn't see what I saw.

I crash into a wall while flying down the stairs. I trip over myself at some point and a slight twinge flashes through my ankle. I run past someone and almost knock them over. I don't stop until the cold wind is biting at my cheeks again.

What. The fuck. Just happened? Am I dreaming? Did I take something and now I'm hallucinating? Is this some kind of sick, twisted joke?

If I turn around and go back upstairs, they'll be ROFL-ing and yelling "April fools" or some shit. Or better yet, it'll just be Miles, pouring cheap boxed wine with *Drag Race* all cued up on the TV. He'll smile and give me a kiss and we'll settle down on the couch with our dinner. *That* is how this evening is supposed to go. Not whatever crap that's left me on a darkened sidewalk in the middle of the night.

My phone buzzes in my pocket and I scramble to pull it out.

> MILES
>
> Babe, come back. Please. It's not what you think.

> WYATT
>
> Connor, I'm really sorry. We need to talk.

Nope. No fucking way. Absolutely not. My hands tremble as I shut the phone off and stuff it into my pocket again. I am not going back up there. Not tonight.

Maybe not ever.

Their faces. Fuck, their faces are burned into my fucking retinas. Guilty, but not the right kind of guilty. Mortified that they'd gotten caught, but not sorry for fucking each other behind my back.

Jesus. I've been living with Miles for over a year now. I fall asleep and wake up next to him almost every goddamn day. Wyatt has been my ride-or-die since the first day of film school. We've gotten drunk together, high together, laid together. We've pulled countless all-nighters, eating cold pizza at three in the morning. They're the two most important people in my life, the ones I turn to when shit hits the fan.

Even now, when they're the shit that's hit my fan, my first instinct is still to call up one of them and tell them what happened.

Except, they aren't the people I thought they were. The boyfriend I know and the best friend I have would never do that to me. They wouldn't lie to me and betray my trust and do it all right under my fucking nose. In my apartment—the one I spent months looking for when Miles wanted us to move in together. In my goddamn bed.

And where else? The couch, the shower, the kitchen counter? If my stomach wasn't already empty, I might just hurl. Bile burns in my chest either way.

I straggle down the street. My legs are already useless from the spin class and now the cold helps numb them even more. But nothing can mute the riot in my head. Questions and accusations and denials crash into each other until I want to scream at the top of my lungs. Maybe then I'll wake up and find that this is all a horrible, very bad nightmare.

I walk. My feet take me down streets and around corners until there's a bright storefront beside me. I wrench the door open and stumble inside. Warm stale air, sharp and tangy like air isn't supposed to be, assaults my nose. I push back the hood of my coat and stare at my surroundings.

I'm at Mars Fitness.

"Hey, Connor."

I flinch. My name doesn't sound like mine anymore.

My body doesn't feel like mine either. The life I thought I had less than an hour ago was a sham and now I don't trust anything.

"What's up? You forget something?" Sawyer eyes me curiously from behind the front desk.

Donnie's at the far end. He's changed from his cycling gear into a staff t-shirt, the Mars logo a bright crest on his chest. Black-rimmed glasses are perched on his nose and he's tapping a pen on a stack of papers.

Oh god. What am I doing here? I need to leave. I need to hide.

My feet stay planted exactly where they are.

I need to pretend I'm okay so they won't guess what happened. Can they tell by looking at me? Do I have it written across my face?

I open my mouth and the sound that comes out isn't human. It's a cross between a dying duck and nails on the chalkboard. My vision goes blurry and suddenly, the floor is rushing at me. I make it halfway down before strong arms come out of nowhere and catch me.

DONNIE

One minute, he's standing there like he can't figure out how he got here. The next, he's swan diving toward the floor. If I was standing even one foot farther away, I would never have made it to him in time.

"Oh, shit!" Sawyer shouts from behind the front desk. "Is he okay?"

I'm on my knees with this guy and his puffy winter coat in my lap. He's simultaneously hyperventilating and sobbing. He's having some sort of attack. My guess is that he's not okay. Not by a long shot.

"What did you say his name was?"

"Connor. His name's Connor." Sawyer somehow knows the name of every single member of the gym, which is mind-boggling to me, but that's what makes him so great at his job.

I'm not so great with names, I'm better with faces. And I've seen Connor in my spin class before. Just earlier tonight, in fact. He was in his usual spot in the back corner and he'd seemed fine. I hadn't noticed any signs of distress or overexertion. He'd looked good at the end of class when I did my personal check-ins with each person.

"Hey, Connor, buddy. You want to stand up for me? So we can get out of the way?" It's getting late so the gym isn't all that busy, but we're right in front of the door and there are already a few people hovering around us, rubbernecking the action.

Connor is about my height, but he's got broad shoulders and probably a good fifty pounds on me. I wave Sawyer over to help me get him to his feet. The staff break room is behind the front desk, so we maneuver him back there and out of sight of the curious onlookers.

He clings to me the entire time like he can't stand up on his own, and when I try to deposit him on the couch, he won't let me go. I have no choice but to sit with him, holding him as great big sobs wrack his body. His hands are fisted in my shirt and his face is plastered to my shoulder. Hot, wet tears soak through to my skin.

His crying is making my heart hurt. They're soul-shattering, coming from deep inside, ripping through him like they're trying to turn him inside out. I know what those kinds of cries feel like. I know how your mind goes blank and the only thing that's real is the excruciating pain. How you want to scream and tear things apart because that's the only way to keep the pain from destroying you.

I've spent the past three years cycling in and out of crying sessions like this. Watching someone else go through it is almost as hard as going through it myself. "Shh, it's okay. Let it out. I've got you."

My thumb slides across my palm to spin my wedding ring around my finger. It's hard to believe it's been three years already. Well, closer to four now. During those first few months after Roger died, I spent every day like this. I lay in bed for days on end, drenching my pillow in tears. Even when I managed to come back to work, I had to run into the staff showers whenever the grief got too much and stick my face under the water in case I suddenly burst into tears. I still feel it sometimes, the need to exhaust myself with sobbing whenever the pain gets overwhelming.

I take a deep breath, then another. I'm shaking almost as hard as Connor is. It's impossible not to feel the misery rolling off him, to not internalize it a little bit.

"Is he okay?" Sawyer whispers as he crouches down in front of us with a box of tissues.

I almost want to send him for paper towels instead. Those tissues aren't going to cut it. I nod toward the refrigerator. "Grab some Gatorade."

Connor's going to be very dehydrated after all this crying and he's already been sweating all evening from my class. He's going to need all the electrolytes I can pour into him.

"Got it."

I shift Connor in my arms and settle a little deeper into the couch. It's awkward since Connor is bigger than me and he's still wearing his puffy winter coat. Even then, he has somehow managed to curl himself into a small ball against my chest. His great big, heaving sobs have dried up, leaving him trembling and weak. I tighten my arms around him, and he relaxes into me.

Sawyer comes back with the Gatorade and a trash bin. "You going to be okay with him for a bit? I gotta take care of a couple things."

I nod to Sawyer and he disappears out the door.

There're a few minutes of silence, then Connor hiccups. I bite my lip to smother a smile. There's nothing funny about crying so hard it triggers involuntary muscle spasms in his diaphragm. Except Connor's a big guy and the sound that comes out of his throat is tiny, almost cute. It eases some of the discomfort in my heart from watching him cry. He's coming out of it. He's going to be okay.

He hiccups again.

"Sorry," he mutters.

"It's not a problem." I hold out a few tissues for him and he sits up to blow his nose. It's loud and snotty and he needs several more before his sinuses are clear. He ends up with a miniature mountain of soiled tissues that he dumps into the trash.

I crack open the cap on a bottle of Gatorade and push it into his hands. "Here. Drink this. You're going to get a headache if you don't keep yourself hydrated."

Connor grips the bottle with both hands and the blue-colored liquid sloshes around inside from how much he's still shaking. He sips at it, taking small, dainty slurps. His eyes are red and starting to get puffy. His eyelashes are dark and clumped together with tears. His cheeks are still damp and his bottom lip sticks out in a little pout that makes him look more like a boy than a man.

He's stiff beside me, sitting at an odd angle, like he doesn't want to pull away entirely but he doesn't know if he's allowed to lean on me again. His leg is pressed against mine, and I'm running my hand up and down his back.

He peeks over his shoulder at me and freezes like a

deer when he meets my gaze. "You're Donnie, The Spin Instructor."

My smile is pained. I'm really not a fan of the moniker, I don't even know where it came from. It's not the spin instructor part, it's the way people say it, like "spin instructor" is actually "sex instructor" or something. My colleagues love it though, and I've caught them referring to me that way with members like it's my official job title.

"Sorry." Connor's eyes flick to my shoulder. "I ruined your shirt." He sounds so goddamn miserable that the soreness in my heart comes back.

I lean forward and reach my arm around him to nudge him closer. He takes the invitation and tucks himself against me again. "It's just a shirt," I say. "I've got plenty more."

I tap on the bottle Connor's holding and he lifts it to his lips for another drink. I keep my breathing slow and steady, and eventually, Connor starts to match my rhythm. The tension melts away from his body and his eyes blink like they're too heavy to keep open.

I want to card my fingers through his hair. I want to press my lips to his temple. I want to tuck him into bed and hold him until he falls asleep. The urge to take care of him knocks me back a bit. I haven't felt this impulse since Roger's big baby antics whenever he fell ill. It must be the intensity of Connor's emotions that's triggering all my protective caretaker tendencies. He's a wreck and I can't just stand by and do nothing.

Sawyer comes back, pulling a chair next to the couch to sit with us. He asks me a silent question with his eyes and I try to give him a reassuring smile in return.

"Dude," he speaks softly to Connor. "You okay?"

Connor doesn't respond. His eyes are open, so I assume he heard.

"Do you want to tell us what happened?" I ask. "Maybe there's something we can do to help?"

He recoils and starts shaking again.

"It's okay. It's all right. You don't have to tell us if you don't want to." I rub my hand vigorously up and down his arm to chase away the trembles. "Whatever it is, it'll all get sorted. I promise."

Connor sniffles and it sounds like he's crying again.

"Shh, I've got you. It's okay." I keep murmuring all the encouraging words I can think of.

"It… hurts…" He speaks so softly I feel the words against my neck more than I hear them.

They break my heart. I crush him to me like I can physically squeeze the pain out of him. He leans into it, soaking up everything I'm giving him until I feel like we're vibrating on the same wavelength. His pain is leeching into me and I'm sending back comfort, and we go back and forth, back and forth.

I'm crying now, my tears rolling down my cheeks and dripping off my jaw into Connor's hair. His hands are in my shirt again, gripping so hard, he might rip it. We're both shaking and there's nothing we can do except ride it out.

Sawyer's sitting there, chewing on his lip while staring at us, horrified and helpless. He glances at the big ticking clock on the wall. "It's almost time to close up."

Shit, it is. We need to clear everyone out so the cleaning crew can go through the place. I blink back my tears.

"Connor, is there someone we can call for you? Or somewhere you can go?"

He shakes his head against my shoulder. "No, I can't. I can't."

"Okay, okay." I'm quick to reassure him. He doesn't have anywhere to go and he can't stay here all night. There's only one other option I can think of. "Do you want to come home with me?"

Sawyer's eyebrows shoot up to his hairline. Connor turns into a statue in my arms.

"I have a guest room," I say quickly. "You can stay there for tonight. Or a few nights. However long you need. It's got its own bathroom and I've got spare towels and toothbrushes—the whole works."

My pulse is racing like I've dodged a car door opening into the bike lane. I can't believe the words that have come out of my mouth.

Connor pulls away just enough to look up at me. His face is a mess of tears and snot and splotchy skin. "Are you sure?" He sounds so small, so fragile, like he'll fall apart again at the slightest touch.

I throw all the confidence I don't feel into my voice. "Yeah, of course. I have friends stay with me all the time. It's no big deal."

It's a big fat lie, is what it is. I haven't had anyone in that guest room in years. I've barely had anyone in the house with me at all. Sawyer's staring at me like I've got horns growing out of my head, but what other choice do we have?

Connor's bottom lip pushes out again and he ducks his head. I can almost hear his thoughts whirling around in there. Should he trust Donnie, The Spin Instructor? Or should he take his chances elsewhere?

"Okay," he finally says. "Maybe just for a few days."

I let out the breath I didn't realize I'm holding, only for my lungs to fill with panic. Oh god, I haven't had anyone in that guest room in literal years. The only people besides me who have been inside the house are random tradespeople I've called to fix things I don't know how to fix myself. Is that bathroom clean? Are the sheets on the bed fresh? I think I left dishes in the kitchen sink this morning. I'm not ready for a houseguest.

No, keep your shit together, Donnie. Now is not the time to freak out. Connor needs steady and stable, not manic fretting over an imperfect house.

"Good. Great." My voice is a whole lot stronger than my quivering insides. "I've got a few things to finish up, then we can head out. Can you hang out here for a bit?"

Connor hesitates, like he'd rather follow me around the gym than be left alone. I give his arm a firm squeeze before setting him away from me.

"Don't worry. I'll be quick."

He shrinks back into the couch. "Okay."

"Good. Good. Great." I wish I had blankets to tuck around him to keep him safe and warm, but he'll have to make do until we get home.

Sawyer follows me out of the break room. "Are you sure this is a good idea, Donnie?"

"Do you have a better one?" The pen I dropped when I went to catch Connor is on the floor and I scoop it up to finish filling out my daily logs.

Sawyer chews on his lip. "Not really."

"It's only for a few days." I try to write, and my letters look like I'm a five-year-old learning how to hold a pencil.

"What if he's, like, a serial killer?"

I cock an eyebrow at Sawyer. "A serial killer?"

"Okay, maybe not a serial killer, but you know what I mean. What if he's, like… unstable or something?"

He's not. I don't know how I know—I just do. Connor's hurting. He needs someone. I want to be that someone. I haven't been more sure of anything in a really long time.

"If I don't show up tomorrow," I say to Sawyer, only half joking. "Send Beau and Gavin to look for me."

The two owners of Mars have been my closest friends for years. Beau's also a big hulking dude and the three of us should be able to wrestle Connor to the ground if it comes to that. It won't, but at least we have a contingency plan in place.

CONNOR

Donnie lives in a brownstone. That's all I register as I follow him up the stoop and into the house. I let him take my coat from me and hang it on the rack by the door. He leads me past a few rooms to the back of the house where he deposits me on a stool next to the kitchen island.

I'm a zombie. Dead and alive at the same time, my body is nothing more than a shell of flesh. My feet move me to where I'm supposed to go. My legs sit me down where I'm supposed to sit. I don't control them, I don't even feel them. I don't feel anything, not even the rage that consumed me at Mars.

Back there, my body had been too small to contain all the shit rioting around inside me. Anger, sadness, disbelief, more anger, at Miles and Wyatt. At myself. They multiplied and multiplied until they burst out of me in those fucking awful sobs. It felt like I was trying to heave my guts out. It kinda feels like I'd succeeded.

"Here, drink all of that." Donnie sets a new bottle of

Gatorade in front of me, the cap already missing. The blue liquid looks like toilet bowl cleaner. "You need to hydrate or you'll wake up with a massive headache tomorrow."

I already have a headache, a steady throbbing of my brain against the inside of my skull. I don't think toilet bowl cleaner is going to make it go away, but what the hell do I know? I drink the Gatorade.

"I'm guessing you haven't had dinner yet, have you?" Donnie asks. He's moving around the kitchen, opening cabinets and shutting drawers. Every clang and every bang is reverberating through the sludge in my head, making the throbbing across my forehead worse.

Dinner. My tacos are on the floor of the apartment. Shame floods through me and I bury my face in my hands. God, what the fuck. I have to be dreaming. This has to be a nightmare.

I'm sitting in Donnie, The Spin Instructor's kitchen. He's trying to make me dinner. I was supposed to be having dinner with my boyfriend, but I'm not because he's fucking my best friend. I'm missing my tacos and wishing I hadn't dropped them before running out of the building.

How is this real? Fucking tacos. Who the fuck cares about tacos or dinner or fucking eating? Instead of fixating on tacos, maybe I should've been more focused on what my boyfriend and best friend were doing right under my fucking nose. Maybe then, I wouldn't be sitting in Donnie, The Spin Instructor's kitchen like a sad, pathetic loser.

"Hey."

I jerk up as Donnie's hand closes over my wrist.

"I'm going to make some salmon and roasted vegetables, okay? Are you allergic to anything?"

I shake my head. "I'm not very hungry."

His brows draw together. "You need to eat something, even if it's only a couple of bites. You've burned a lot of calories tonight and you need to keep your blood sugar up." He pushes the half-empty bottle of Gatorade into my hand again. "And you have to finish this."

My wrist is cold when he lets go of it. Just like my whole body had felt cold when he left me in that room to go do whatever it was he needed to do before we left Mars. I want his hand on my wrist again. I want his arms around me again. I didn't feel cold then. I didn't tremble so much when he held me. I'd been floating aimlessly, set adrift, and then Donnie pulled me in and anchored me. I want to feel anchored again.

Donnie slides a tray into the oven and sets a timer. Then he turns to me, arm outstretched. I go to him and nestle into his side. His calm settles over me and I can breathe again.

"Come on. Let me show you to your room. You can wash your face and change into something more comfortable. Dinner will be ready when you come back down."

Donnie grabs my bag from where I dropped it by the front door and we go up to the second floor. He ushers me into the guest room and I do nothing but stand there by the corner of the bed, not sure what comes next. Donnie sets my bag on a padded bench at the foot of the bed.

"Do you have anything to change into?"

I stare at my bag. The only things in there are my laptop and the sweaty clothes I took off after his class. Everything else I own is at the apartment. I have literally nothing but the clothes on my back. My throat closes up and I sit heavily on the edge of the bed. How is this fucking real?

"No? Okay. Not a problem."

Donnie disappears and I stare at the floor. There's an area rug on top of the hardwood. It's beige-y and shaggy and I wiggle my toes in it. I've always wanted a rug like this in my bedroom so I can feel the soft squishiness under my feet when I get up in the morning. Guess I have my chance now.

My head spins and I suck in a breath. I'd forgotten to breathe.

Donnie comes back with a stack of fluffy white towels, neatly-folded flannel PJs, socks, and a toothbrush and toothpaste. He tilts his head for me to follow him. "Bathroom's over here."

It's one of the other doors that open off the landing of the second floor. Donnie sets his stack of linens on the counter and turns to me.

"You all right?"

They keep asking me that and I keep not knowing what to say. No, I'm not all right, not really. But I'm all right enough, I guess. I don't know. I don't know what I'm supposed to be.

Donnie flinches and shakes his head in a jerking motion. "Never mind. Pretend I didn't ask that. Wash your face—or you can take a shower if you'd like. These pajamas are clean and I think should fit you. Come back downstairs when you're ready."

He squeezes past me and I get a whiff of something woodsy and citrusy. I follow it to Donnie at the bathroom door. He's got the doorknob in his hand and he's pulling it shut. I almost stop him so I can take in a little more of that comforting scent.

He closes the door, and I lean my forehead against it.

God, I'm tired. I want to curl up in a ball, bury my nose in the crook of Donnie's neck, and fall asleep breathing him in. It's the only thing that makes any sense—Donnie, his hugs, his scent—everything else feels like one fucked up nightmare that I desperately want to wake up from.

I push away from the door and turn on the faucet to splash water on my face. It's cold and the shock of it jolts me back into my body. I can feel how swollen my eyes are, how raw my throat is. The headache throbs even stronger and the room looks like it spinning.

I splash my face a few more times before turning the water off. I'm more awake now, but I'm not sure that's a good thing. Maybe being a zombie is better than being able to catalog every single thing that's wrong.

The PJs are soft, though they smell a little like mothballs. Donnie must've pulled them out of a bottom drawer somewhere. They fit me, almost like they were bought for me, and I'm immediately warmer after I put them on. The socks are thick and fluffy and feel like heaven on my feet.

Donnie's pulling the tray out of the oven when I get back down to the kitchen. Whatever he's made smells amazing and my stomach growls in anticipation. I still don't really feel like eating, but my body apparently has ideas of its own.

"Go ahead and sit down." Donnie nods toward a table by the window.

It's dark outside and the light from the kitchen reflects off the glass. The table already has two place settings laid out and I drop into the chair in front of one. God, I'm so tired.

"You're crashing." Donnie sets a plate down in front of me.

There's a pale pink slice of salmon, stalks of asparagus, and chunks of zucchini and tomatoes. It looks like something off an Instagram reel.

"Huh?" I blink at Donnie.

"You've been running on adrenaline for the past couple hours, and now you're crashing."

"Oh." That makes a lot of sense actually. I kinda want to sleep for a week.

"Eat as much as you can, and then we'll get you to bed."

I pick up the fork and it clatters against the plate. If Donnie notices, he doesn't say anything. I grip the fork harder, but that only makes the shaking worse. I manage to stab a piece of zucchini and shove it into my mouth. My tastebuds register that it tastes good. My stomach rumbles in appreciation. I force myself to take another bite.

What are Miles and Wyatt eating? Are they helping themselves to my tacos? Are they watching *Drag Race* without me? I choke on a flake of salmon that wants to go down the wrong way.

Donnie hands me the glass of water I didn't notice was sitting right there. "Take it easy. Just a little at a time."

"It's Miles and Wyatt." The words slip out of my mouth and I hear them like I'm listening to the conversation from the other side of the room.

"Who?"

"Boyfriend and best friend." I frown. "Ex-boyfriend. Ex-best friend."

"What did they do?"

"They're fucking. Each other." My chest hurts. It feels like there's a boulder sitting on it.

Donnie winces. "Fuck. I'm sorry."

"Yeah." My voice is tight. I'm not breathing. "Me too."

"You just found out?"

I nod. "When I got ho—back to the apartment."

Donnie's hand closes over mine and I grip it hard. It's my lifeline, my tether. I'm drifting and it's the only thing keeping me here, keeping me sane.

"You're here now. You're at my house, with me. You can stay here for as long as you want. You don't have to go back there."

I'm here. With Donnie. He's going to let me stay. I'm safe here. Nothing bad can happen to me while I'm here.

I manage to eat a bit more and finish off the salmon and half the vegetables. Donnie watches me the entire time and his expression brightens with every bite I swallow. He's proud of me. I want that gold star. I take another bite.

"Good job," he says when I set the fork down, and a little bit of that giddy happy feeling I get at the end of spin class trickles through the muck in my brain. I think I even eke out a smile.

"Go on up to bed," Donnie says.

I look at him. Donnie, The Sexy Spin Instructor. Salt and pepper hair, faint lines across his forehead and at the corners of his eyes. He's got stubble all along his jaw.

"Thank you," I whisper. For dinner, for giving me a place to crash, for holding me while I melted down, for not getting upset when I ruined his shirt. I don't know what I would've done if he hadn't been at Mars. I suck in a gasping breath and hold it in my lungs.

"You're welcome. Now go to bed."

I nod, stand, and climb the stairs. Because Donnie, The Spin Instructor, told me to. And Donnie, The Spin Instructor knows what to do.

DONNIE

I wait for Connor to get upstairs before I let the air out of my lungs in one giant *whoosh*. Fuck. Connor's crashing and I'm crashing right along with him. It's been an intense evening, even for me.

My hands are a little unsteady as I clear the table and I set the plates down by the sink to grip the edge of the kitchen counter. Deep breaths. In and hold. Out and hold. It takes several cycles for my pulse to slow to a more manageable rate.

I fill the tea kettle and turn it on. I'm going to need some tea in order to get to sleep tonight.

It's not only Connor and the shitty evening he's had. It's me and all the feelings bubbling to the surface because Connor is in the house, sleeping in the guest room, wearing Roger's clothes.

I squeeze my eyes shut. I was up in the walk-in closet when I realized Connor was never going to fit into my clothes. He's so much wider than I am. But about the same size Roger was. It paralyzed me for a good few seconds as all the grief and sorrow around losing Roger came crashing down on me. A sharp pain exploded in my chest and I had to lean against the wall to keep from collapsing to the floor.

I haven't felt it so acutely in a while now, that gut-wrenching pain that makes it impossible to breathe, impossible to move, that makes me want to die so it won't hurt so much anymore. It's the same kind of sobbing I'd held Connor through at Mars. Except his pain is fresh and I've already had almost four years to deal with mine.

He needed something to wear. My clothes wouldn't fit him. So that left Roger's. I forced myself to cross to Roger's side of the walk-in closet where most of his clothes still sit, exactly where they would've been if he was still with me. His pajamas are in a built-in dresser and the first set on top was a nice plaid flannel in deep forest green. I have a matching set in light blue. We got them during a ski trip to Vermont when I forgot to pack pajamas for us.

They fit Connor well. Almost too well. The top stretches perfectly across his broad shoulders, the bottoms are just snug enough around the hips to hint at a great ass. I almost dropped the baking tray full of our dinner when he walked into the kitchen.

I dunk the dishes into the hot soapy water in the sink. I'm not used to having anyone else in the kitchen. The last time I had people in here was... Roger's wake. There'd been so many people—our friends, Roger's parents, his colleagues. The counter was covered with dishes wrapped in aluminum foil. The fridge could barely close with how full it was.

I dropped a plate that day and it shattered on the

kitchen floor. I'm still not sure whether it slipped out of my hand by accident or if I purposefully let it go. After that first one, I wanted to smash all the plates. I would have if Roger's father, Leonard, hadn't pushed me out of the kitchen.

I still remember what it felt like to be in the house that day, so vividly that sometimes it feels like it was yesterday. The weight of Roger's death was so heavy, so crushing, I collapsed under it. It's taken me a long time to figure out how to live with that weight. I'm better at it now, better at carrying it, better at hiding how heavy it is.

I give the kitchen one last wipe down, then make myself a mug of chamomile tea and bring it upstairs with me. I stop on the second-floor landing. The door to the guest room is open and the light is still on. When I peek inside, I find Connor lying on his side in the middle of the bed, on top of the covers.

He looks so small like that, so defenseless and vulnerable. This big guy, all curled up, his thick thighs tucked against his chest. His dark blond hair is all tousled and his lip is pushed out in that pout.

I set my hand on his shoulder and give him a shake. "Connor."

His eyes flutter open and reveal light brown irises that remind me of caramel. Warm and sweet and comforting. He stares at me, but I'm not sure if he sees me at all.

"Come on, let's get you under the covers." I set my mug aside and tug Connor to his feet.

He moves slowly, loose and languid. He's probably on the edge of unconsciousness. I get him onto the bed, head on a pillow, and drag the covers over him, making sure they're wrapped snuggly around him. When I turn to go, his arm shoots out from under the bedding and latches onto my wrist.

"Don't leave." His words are slurred with fatigue, but the neediness in them is as clear as a bell. It echoes through me and I can't tell whether I'm reflecting what he's projecting or whether I need that comfort too. Either way, I can't leave him.

I climb onto the bed next to him, the thickness of the covers separating us. Connor immediately molds himself to me, head on my shoulder, arm flung across my body. He rubs his cheek back and forth, breathing in deep like he's filling himself up on my smell. When he sighs, all the tension melts away and he's heavy and soft on top of me.

His weight… I close my eyes as my body pushes through the murkiness of a four-year slumber. His hair tickles my chin, his chest rises and falls against my side, his arm is heavy on my stomach, his hand is curled possessively around my hip. I haven't slept next to anyone since Roger. Hell, I haven't held anyone as closely as I've held Connor since then either.

My brain dumps barrels and barrels of oxytocin into my system, the entire stockpile over the last four years. It feels so goddamn good to have Connor on me, touching me, curled up around me. My skin is all sensitive and tingly. My muscles are liquid like I've had a deep tissue massage. And my dick… Christ, my dick roars to life.

I'm hard, achingly hard. From something as simple as having a guy cuddle me in bed. We're both fully clothed. There's a thick blanket between us. But all my dick cares about is that I have a man on top of me and it feels fucking good.

Connor is already asleep. He was out the second I laid

down with him. The ten extra minutes I stay there are for me. Only me. I let myself enjoy his weight, the softness of his hair, the scent of Mars's locker room soap that still clings to his skin. I let myself soak it all in, as much of it as I can get, until I'm almost falling asleep myself.

Then I ease myself out from under him. I collect my now-cold mug, turn off the lights, and close the door behind me without a backward glance. It was nice. I needed that. But I didn't bring Connor back here so I could take advantage of his body while he is unconscious.

I go upstairs and turn the water on for a shower. Under the spray, I close my eyes and run my soapy hands over my still-tingly skin. My dick sticks out from my body and I gasp when I wrap my fingers around it. I'm so sensitive— I'm so *hard*—I'm almost afraid to touch myself for fear of ending this too soon.

My balls hang heavy between my legs and I fondle them, tugging them down and away. The light pain reels me back from the edge and I give myself a couple strokes. *Yeeesss.* My entire body shudders as all my pleasure receptors fire.

I imagine Roger behind me, his big body covering my back. He reaches around me and it's his hand on my cock, his hand on my balls. I tilt my head back, water falling on my face, sluicing down my body. Roger squeezes tight, exactly the way I like it, concentrating his strokes near the head of my dick. Heat pools in my groin, a pressure that builds faster than I would like. But I can't hold it back this time, it's rushing at me too quickly. My balls draw up and there's a moment where I hover on the edge, where that one moment stretches into eternity, then I'm falling.

The orgasm crashes through me, bursting out of my

cock in thick ropes of cum. I milk myself until I feel weak in the knees, then nestle into the broad chest against my back. I sigh and turn my head for a kiss. The imaginary lips that find mine aren't Roger's. They're Connor's.

My eyes snap open and I slap my hand against the wall to brace myself. Jesus Christ. My body is still all light and floaty, my head a little dizzy from the steam filling the bathroom. Guilt, thick and cloying, seeps into me and I hurry out of the shower.

It was Roger in my fantasy. Not Connor. Roger—not Connor.

Except Roger had a beard and the man in my imagination was clean-shaven. Roger was a few inches taller than me and the man behind me was my height. Roger's lips were wide and the lips that touched mine were plumper, poutier.

I rush through brushing my teeth, throw some moisturizer on my face, and pull on my own set of pajamas—not the light blue set. I climb into the king-sized bed and reach across to where Roger used to lie next to me. There's so much space, so much cold bedding. I feel so small in the middle of it. I squeeze my eyes shut against the guilt and pleasure fighting for space inside me.

I don't know which one I should feel or which one is the right reaction to have. The only thing I know is that I've felt the weight of Connor's body against mine. And I want more.

CONNOR

Ugh. I'm hot. Sweaty. I'm trapped in a tangle of blankets and *uggghhh*. Oh, wait.

I open my eyes to an unfamiliar ceiling. I'm not at home. This is not my bed.

It all comes flooding back into my head. Going home. Finding Miles and Wyatt. Running out of the apartment and somehow ending up at Mars.

Donnie.

He brought me to his house and everything after that is kinda fuzzy. There had been salmon, incredibly soft pajamas—the ones that are currently trying to smother me —and getting wrapped up in something that felt so comfortable and safe.

I kick the blankets away and reach down to strip the fuzzy socks off my feet. I immediately feel ten degrees cooler. The flannel I put on last night had been warm and cuddly, but now it's damp and every inch of me feels gross. I push myself up and a jackhammer goes off in my head.

"Ah, fuck." I press the heel of my hand against my forehead, waiting for the pounding to fade. I haven't had a hangover like this since… film school? Nope, no, not going there. No thinking about film school or anything to do with Wyatt or Miles.

Moving slowly, I swing my legs over the side of the bed and notice a bottle of Gatorade on the nightstand. Of course, hydrate. Donnie did say something about needing to drink more Gatorade. I down half the bottle, the sickly-sweet liquid clinging to my morning tongue. "Yuck."

I need to brush my teeth, but I only make it as far as the floor. My ankle flashes with pain when I try to step on it and I end up in a pile of limbs and sweaty flannel beside the bed. "Fuck, Jesus, what the hell?"

Footsteps fly up the stairs. "Are you okay?"

Donnie is on me, running his hands all over me like he's searching for injuries.

"Yeah, I think so?" I'm holding my ankle with one hand and bracing my head with the other, waiting for the spiky throbs to die down.

"What happened?" Donnie takes my foot into his hand and gently moves his fingers over the joints of my ankle. "Your ankle wasn't injured yesterday, was it?"

"I don't know. Maybe?" The flash of pain is familiar though. Oh, right. "I think I stepped on it wrong when I was… running down the stairs." Trying to escape the horror show that was unfolding in the apartment.

"It didn't hurt yesterday?"

"It did, initially. And then it didn't until just now."

Donnie nods. "Probably the adrenaline. It masked the pain so you could deal with it later. Can you get up?"

"Yeah." I take the hand he offers and let him pull me to my feet—foot. I sit down on the bed and wince as my head throbs again.

"Headache?" Donnie asks.

"Yeah."

"It's because you're de—"

"Dehydrated. I know." I smile and point to the half-empty bottle on the nightstand. "Thank you for that."

Donnie gives me a stern look. "Finish the rest of that while I get you some Aspirin and ice."

I really want to brush my teeth first to get rid of the fuzz on my tongue, but I do as he says and polish off the rest of the bottle. Now my bladder is protesting and I shift uncomfortably. Fuck it—I need the bathroom.

I'm cautious as I test out my ankle. It's not so bad if I step on it gingerly and don't put too much weight on it. I hobble to the bathroom without falling on my face and even manage to pee standing up.

Donnie's waiting for me in the bedroom with a glass of water, a bottle of Aspirin, and a bag of peas. He shakes two tablets onto my hand and holds out the glass of water for me. He eyes me while I swallow the pills down.

"Do you want to shower before we ice your ankle?"

I must look as gross as I feel. "Yeah, please."

He stays close as I inch my way toward the bathroom, like he's afraid I'm going to collapse under my own weight. "You'll be okay in there? You're not going to slip in the shower?"

"I'll be fine. It doesn't even hurt if I'm standing still." Although, if he's offering to come into the shower with me… "Really, I'm good. Thanks." I give myself a mental smack in the head. No coming on to the spin instructor. Not when he's been nothing but kind and generous. It's like I've completely forgotten that I had a boyfriend as recently as twelve hours ago.

"Okay, shout if you need anything. I'll bring your breakfast up." Donnie shuts the door for me, maybe a little quicker than necessary.

The shower feels fucking amazing. It's one of those rainwater showerheads that pour water directly on top of my head and I stand there letting it wash everything away. All the icky sweat and all the fuzzy shit on my tongue. I wish I could wash Miles and Wyatt away too, the hurt, the betrayal, the rejection. If only.

Even then, I feel about a thousand percent better when I get out of the shower. Except now my choices are to hang out in Donnie's house naked or wear yesterday's clothes. I *really* don't want to wear yesterday's clothes.

With a towel wrapped around my waist, I go back to the guest room and find a pair of sweats and a t-shirt waiting for me on the padded bench. Donnie again, always thinking of things two steps ahead of me. I'm pulling the t-shirt on when there's a knock on the door.

Donnie has a tray of food. Coffee, orange juice, a banana, an apple, and omg, a stack of pancakes. There's even a little jar of what looks like milk and a packet of sweetener on the tray. This is legit room service level of pampering.

"Whoa." I step back and let Donnie in. "Is that all for me?"

"I figured you'd be hungry." He sets the tray down on the spot where he left the clothes, then goes to rearrange the pillows on the bed. "Sit down and prop your foot up on this."

I really don't think I need to ice the ankle, but it's his house and he's the spin instructor, so I do as he says. He balances the bag of peas over my ankle, then brings the tray over and slides it carefully onto the bed.

"I didn't know how you liked your coffee."

"With lots of milk and sugar."

He stares in shock as I dump all the milk and sweetener into the mug. "That's more milk and sweetener than coffee."

"Just the way I like it!" I take a sip and yeah, that's the spot. Honestly, I'd be happy with just this. He didn't need to bring up all the extra stuff. Still—pancakes. I pick up the fork and knife and cut into the small stack.

"Those are protein pancakes."

I stop with the fork in my mouth. Whatever I've taken a bite of, it's not a pancake.

Donnie snickers from where he's sitting at the end of the bed. "Egg whites, low-fat cottage cheese, rolled oats, and a honey drizzle. You can slice the banana on top if you'd like."

I chew. It's not bad. It's not a pancake, but I've eaten worse shit as a college student. I swallow and wash it down with my milk and sweetener with a dash of coffee.

"It's healthy for you. You get used to it." Donnie says with a smirk.

I mean, if eating protein pancakes every day gives me a body like Donnie's, then… yeah, no, I'll stick with my chonky figure, thanks. I cut another piece of pancake because now that I know what to expect, it's pretty decent.

"I have to go to work in a bit," Donnie says, sobering. "Do you have any plans for today?"

What day is it today? It kinda feels like a week's passed since my life got upended, except that was only yesterday. Which makes today Saturday. "No, not today."

"Good. You shouldn't be going anywhere on that ankle anyway." He adjusts the bag of peas to keep it from sliding off my foot. "Will you be okay staying here by yourself?"

"Yeah, I'll be fine. You don't need to worry about me. I'll start looking for a place to stay so I can get out of your hair."

A look comes over Donnie's face, a little dark, a little annoyed, almost offended. "You don't need to do that. You're welcome to stay for as long as you need. It's not like I'm using the space for anything else."

That's true. The place is freakishly large for just one person. Except Donnie's wearing a wedding ring and he's twirling it around his finger. Has he always worn the ring? I've never noticed it before, but then, I've never made a point to look.

"Do you… live here by yourself?" It's the nicest way I can think of to ask. I haven't seen anyone else in the house and I've never heard of Donnie, The Spin Instructor, having a husband, but that doesn't mean he doesn't have one.

Donnie slides his hand under his thigh, like he's forcing himself not to toy with his ring. He looks off to the side before speaking. "Yeah, I do. My husband… died almost four years ago."

Jesus fucking Christ. "Oh my god, I'm so sorry."

Donnie's smile is tight. "Thank you. It was… a long time ago."

From the set of his jaw and the way his brows are drawn slightly together, my guess is it doesn't feel like it was that long ago to Donnie. The sadness coming off him is making my stomach churn and the protein pancakes aren't sitting so well anymore.

"Anyway..." It's obvious he's forcing his smile. His voice is artificially high and bright. "We inherited the house from Roger's great aunt. It was so dilapidated it was practically condemned. We spent two years remodeling the whole thing. That was ten years ago."

His gaze shifts back toward me, to my chest, then stomach, then legs. There's no heat in his eyes and his lips are pressed into a thin, straight line. He's not checking me out, he's... the clothes. He's looking at the clothes I'm wearing.

I glance down. They look like every day t-shirts and sweatpants. Really nice material, way nicer than any of the stuff I own. There's nothing special about them. Unless— oh, shit.

I pluck at the shirt. "Are these... were they..." Ugh, how do I ask the question without sounding like an ungrateful ass?

Donnie nods. "You're almost the exact size as Roger was. I... still have some of his old clothes."

"And the PJs from last night?"

"Those too."

I swallow around the ball of emotion that's suddenly in my throat. Maybe I should feel weird about wearing a dead man's clothing, but it feels more like an honor. Donnie's clearly still grieving his husband and he's still wearing his wedding ring. It can't be easy handing over Roger's things for a stranger to wear.

"Thank you," I say, getting all choked up. My situation with Miles and Wyatt doesn't seem like such a big deal anymore, not compared to Donnie losing his husband. And here I was yesterday, bawling all over him when he's gone through real heartache and real loss. "How long were you together for?"

Donnie takes a deep breath and blinks away the moisture in his eyes. "About eighteen years."

Miles and I had been together for just over two. What was two years next to eighteen? Nothing, that's what it was. Absolutely nothing. Donnie and Roger had owned a house together. They were married. Me and Miles? Now that I'm thinking about it, I'm not sure if I even loved him that much or in that way.

I cared about him a lot, enough to move in with him. But enough to marry him? I recoil at the thought. I don't know if I would've married him. Certainly, not where we were in the relationship. And now, I can't imagine ever wanting to marry him.

"Well, I need to get going." Donnie stands from the bed and I kinda don't want him to go.

I feel more out of place in the house now than I did before I knew about Roger. It feels like I'm trespassing on his territory or something, like I'm taking advantage of him somehow. He's the one who inherited the property, who spent money and time making it into what it is today, but I'm the one walking around and enjoying it. It doesn't seem fair. It doesn't feel right.

At least with Donnie here, I don't feel like one of those home invaders who squat in empty houses while the owners are out of town.

Donnie's by the door, tapping on the doorframe,

running through a list he's made in his mind. "Try not to walk around on your ankle too much, but obviously, I'm not going to force you to stay in bed all day. There's food in the fridge that's easy to heat up. Help yourself to anything that's in there."

He furrows his brow, like he's forgetting something. "Oh, and there's a theater room in the basement if you want to watch movies or whatever. There's a home gym down there too, but I wouldn't recommend you use it."

My ears perk up at the mention of a theater room and maybe I'll work up the courage to go use Donnie's things when he's not home.

"Do you need anything before I go?"

I shake my head, then stop. "What time do you think you'll get back?" I ask, voice small. It's such a stupid question, something a child would ask when they want to know how long they'll need to look out for themselves.

But Donnie smiles, warmly this time. His eyes go soft and they crinkle at the edges. He looks at me like he wants to walk over and hug me. I wouldn't object if he did.

"Around six. I can make dinner when I get back."

Six o'clock. Eight hours. It's a standard work day and yet it feels like eons. I push down the seed of fear and nervousness that's suddenly implanted itself in me. It's only eight hours. I have work I can do. There are movies to watch. I'll be fine.

I smile and try not to look like I'm afraid of being alone. "Have fun at work."

Donnie half turns to leave, but hesitates. He glances back at me for a moment, then he's closing the distance between us. He pulls me into a hug and we hold each other, neither one of us saying a word. It should feel weird

—two grown men, practically strangers, giving each other a hug goodbye—but it feels like the most natural thing in the world.

He holds me until that seed lodged in me dissolves. I can do this. Donnie will be back in no time.

DONNIE

Sawyer waves me down the moment I step foot inside Mars. "Hey, how'd it go? How's Connor?" he asks conspiratorially.

I pause on the public side of the front desk. Connor looks a lot better this morning than he did last night. His eyes were still a bit puffy when I left for work and he could probably use a few more hours of sleep, but he's nowhere near as wrecked as he was when I brought him home.

"He's fine."

Sawyer leans over the front desk to whisper to me. "Is he still at your place?"

"Yes, he is," I whisper back suspiciously. "Why?"

He glances across the lobby to where there's a juice bar. The barista is serving someone and there are a couple of gym members sitting at the small café tables. He lowers his voice even more. "Connor's boyfriend, Miles, came in this morning looking for him."

"What?" Anger boils up inside me, hot and vicious, and every muscle goes taut, like I'm getting ready to pounce. The fucking audacity. How dare he waltz in here thinking he has any right to ask about Connor? "What did you tell him?" I growl.

Sawyer backs away from me with his hands raised. "Whoa, easy. I didn't tell him anything. Just that Connor isn't here, and I don't know where he is."

My pulse is raging with no signs of slowing down. If Miles came looking for Connor once, he can do it again. We have to protect Connor from the monster. He shouldn't have to see Miles's face ever again if he doesn't want to.

"Bro, what's up? Did Connor tell you what happened last night? Does it have something to do with Miles?"

It isn't my story to tell, but I can't get Miles banned from Mars without giving a reason. And I really, *really* want to get Miles banned. I nod toward the staff break room and Sawyer meets me back there.

"What did Miles say? What were his exact words?" I ask.

"He didn't say much. Just that Connor didn't go home last night and now he's looking for him."

"That's all?"

"That's all! I swear! What happened?"

"The fucking bastard," I mutter. He made it sound like he was the good guy, the concerned partner who is looking for his missing boyfriend. Except the missing boyfriend ran from him for a reason and maybe the missing boyfriend doesn't want to be found.

"Who? Miles? What did he do?"

I stalk to the front desk and wake up the computer we

keep there for membership records. "Do we have a persona non grata list?"

Sawyer's peering over my shoulder. "Uh, yeah, but why do we need it?"

"We're banning Miles."

"What? Why? Donnie, tell me what happened!"

I ignore him to dig through my bag for my reading glasses. A member comes out from the back of the gym at the same time and Sawyer immediately switches modes.

"Hey! Did you have a good workout? Awesome! Enjoy the rest of your day!"

When he turns back to me, I've found my glasses and the persona non grata list. "How does this thing work? How do I add someone to it?"

"You can't. Only Beau or Gavin can."

"Who the fuck came up with that idea?"

"They did? I think it's so we can't just add people we don't like."

I nearly throw the mouse across the lobby. "Fuck." I tear my glasses off my face to rub my eyes and pace away from the computer. My adrenaline is spiking, my body is vibrating, and I know this is an overreaction. I force myself to take deep, slow breaths, but they're not helping.

"Bro, what's going on? You're freaking me out."

Beau pops up out of nowhere right then. "Hey, guys, morning."

I ambush him. "I need you to add someone to the persona non grata list." I tug Beau toward the computer and he stares at me like I've been possessed.

"What?"

I slap my glasses back onto my face and point to the

screen. "Here. I need to add someone new. How do I do that?"

Beau looks to Sawyer who shrugs. "Beats me, man. He won't tell me anything."

"Who do you want to add?" Beau asks me, a scowl on his face.

"His name is Miles." I don't know his last name. I don't know what he looks like. I don't know anything about the guy except that he's a fucking douchebag. But Sawyer apparently does. "You know him, right?"

Sawyer takes a step back from me. "Uh, sorta. I've met him before, if that's what you mean. But I don't like, *know* know him."

"That's good enough. What does he look like?"

Sawyer sends Beau a helpless look and Beau steps in between us.

"Donnie, hey." He puts both hands on my arms and grips so tight I'd probably bruise if I wasn't still wearing my winter coat. "Calm down. Breathe."

I curl my hands into fists by my side and fucking breathe. It works this time. Kind of. Enough for the red tinge to fade out of my vision.

"Start from the beginning. Who is this guy and why do we need to ban him from the premises."

"He's Connor's boyfriend."

"And who's Connor?"

"He's a member."

Beau cocks his head to the side. "You're not making a whole lot of sense, Donnie."

"Connor and Miles are both members," Sawyer jumps in. "Connor's more regular. He goes to Donnie's spin classes. I haven't seen Miles here in months. Connor comes in last night, right before closing, and he just collapses. Right there. Just *boom*, on the floor. And he's sobbing, like hysterical crying, tears and snot everywhere. Donnie and I brought him to the break room and then…" He looks at me and gestures vaguely.

I huff because this next part is going to sound bad. "He needed a place to stay, so I let him come home with me last night."

"You what?" Beau nearly shouts. Across the lobby, the juice bar's barista and the gym members are all staring at us, watching the commotion. Beau takes my arm and pushes me toward the break room. "Explain."

"He needed a place to stay and I've got the guest room, so I let him come home with me." I cross my arms and stare Beau down, daring him to say something.

The guy towers over me. He's not the least bit intimated. "You brought a complete stranger home? And he's one of our members?"

Connor doesn't feel like a stranger, not anymore. He feels like… I don't know, a friend? At the very least, an acquaintance. Except the only word that comes to mind is "mine."

The word echoes through me and I almost stagger at how booming it is. Connor isn't mine in any sense of the word. I just met the guy last night. I know nothing about him. He said Miles cheated on him, but there could be more to the story.

I'm pretty sure there isn't though. I'm pretty sure Connor is exactly who he appears to be, and things with Miles are exactly as he says they are. I don't know how I know. I just know, and that's… terrifying.

"We don't have a rule against that." I lift my chin as I speak.

"What? Fraternizing with members?" Beau scoffs. "No, we don't."

"So, what's the problem?" I'm deliberately being obtuse and it's pissing Beau off, but I don't care.

He runs a hand over his face. "Okay, listen, one thing at a time. You want to ban this Miles guy. Fine. Why?"

"Because he's a fucking asshole."

Beau pins me with an impatient look. "That's not good enough and you know it."

I have to tell him. I have no choice. I *want* to tell him, I realize. I want him and Sawyer and everyone in the gym to know what kind of bastard Miles is. It comes out of me like a compulsion I can't stop. "He cheated on Connor, with Connor's best friend. Connor walked in on them last night when he went home."

There, it's out now, and gratification runs through me like I'm fucking high. Beau doesn't look as angry as he should be though. He looks decidedly unimpressed.

"Okay, and?"

I frown. This isn't going the way it's supposed to. "And Connor was distraught. He couldn't go back there, so I took him home with me."

"And you want to ban the boyfriend because…"

"Because he's a cheating bastard!" What about this isn't Beau getting?

Beau sighs and shakes his head. "Donnie, we can't ban someone because they're cheating bastards. If we did that, we'd lose half our membership. Hell, we've got people joining us for the express purpose of sleeping around. Or have you forgotten about the condoms we stock in the locker rooms?"

He's right and I hate it. I fucking hate it. I don't care about all those other assholes and what they're doing in the locker rooms. I care about Connor and what Miles did to him. "So what, are we condoning infidelity now?" I spit out.

It's entirely the wrong thing to say and I can see how wrong it is on Beau's face. Whatever patience he had is running thin now.

"We're not condoning infidelity," Beau says softly, but menacing enough that I shrink back from him. "But we're not the fucking morality police either. As long as everyone's a consenting adult, remember? That's our policy."

"I doubt Connor consented to being cheated on." It slips out. I don't even consciously think it. I want to take it back the second it's out there because Beau is not happy.

His face is dark and if I didn't know him better, I'd be petrified. I'm a little scared as it is. I take a couple steps away from him as my senses go on high alert.

"That's not what I meant and you know it."

Of course I know it. Beau is right. Everything he's saying makes complete sense and under any other circumstances, I'd agree with him one hundred percent. But not when it comes to Connor, apparently. I can't let it go. I want Miles gone so badly it lodges in the middle of my chest and burns.

Beau's expression softens a touch. "If it helps, Sawyer mentioned the boyfriend hasn't been here in a while," he says, still cautious.

"He was here this morning. Asking about Connor," I say through gritted teeth.

Beau nods as if that explains everything. "We don't have to tell him where Connor is. But we can't ban him unless he violates one of our policies."

I'm not going to win this argument and I've got a class I need to get ready for. They're going to get one hell of a workout today. I shrug out of my winter coat and turn to leave. "Yeah, fine, whatever."

"Donnie."

I stop, but I don't turn back to Beau.

"Are you okay?"

I don't know. This kind of reaction isn't normal for me and I feel off balance, off-kilter.

"Gavin and I are always here if you need to talk."

They are. They always have been, especially after Roger died. I'm not being fair to Beau and a trickle of guilt zaps away most of my anger. I slump, the outrage draining out of me, and I glance back over my shoulder. "Yeah, I know. Thanks."

CONNOR

I force myself to finish the breakfast Donnie made for me and then I lie back down on the bed. I haven't turned on my phone since I shut it off last night and honestly, I kinda don't want to turn it on ever again. I don't want to talk to Miles. I don't want to talk to Wyatt. I don't want to hear what they have to say. I don't want to have anything to do with them.

I want them to go throw themselves off a tall building.

Oh, god. I slap my hands over my face. I'm such a fucking horrible person. Who the fuck thinks shit like that? Especially since Roger is actually dead.

I groan and bury my face into a pillow. I'm so angry. Like, deep in my gut, churning lava, consuming-my-soul angry. I hate them. I despise them. The feeling is so potent, so strong that it scares me. I've never felt this way about anyone before. I didn't think I *could* feel this way.

It's such an ugly feeling, so twisted and dirty, and it

terrifies me, but I kinda revel in it at the same time. It gives me a rush, a sick pleasure to think about all the ways I can make Miles and Wyatt hurt. I want them to hurt as badly as they've hurt me. I want them to hurt *more*. I want to teach them a lesson and laugh in their fucking faces when they beg me for forgiveness.

Jesus Christ, I'm a terrible, terrible person. No wonder they cheated on me.

They were probably like, *Connor's a bitch, we don't need him, we're so much better off together, without him, blah, blah, blah.* Maybe they're right. Maybe I am a nasty bitch. I certainly feel like one right now.

I push myself up. I can't lie in bed with nothing to do but think the same thoughts over and over again. *I hate them. Why did they do this to me? I must've done something to deserve this. I hate them.* The thoughts are spinning around in my head, so many of them, so fast that my head's going to explode.

I get up, not sure what I'm doing or where I'm going, I just need to get out of the room. Maybe Donnie has some books lying around, or maybe I'll go downstairs and check out that theater room he mentioned. I grab the bag of peas that's melting on my ankle and stand up to take a few careful steps. It's fine, only hurts at certain angles. Nothing to worry about.

There's a door at the other end of the second-floor landing. It's unlocked and I push it open to peek inside. It's an office with bookshelves, a filing cabinet, and a leather executive chair. The desk is one of those big solid things, complete with an old-fashioned blotter.

I'm halfway across the room to go scan the bookshelf

when I stop short. There's an ancient-looking laptop sitting off to one side of the desk. A corkboard hangs from the wall, next to the bookshelf, cluttered with yellowing birthday cards and photos of Donnie with another man. They look happy together, smiling into each other's eyes.

Is that Roger? I inch forward for a closer look. Donnie looks younger in the photos. There's no salt in his dark hair. The other guy—it has to be Roger—has a shiny bald head and a full lush beard. He's a big guy, taller than Donnie and wide like me. Love and joy radiate out of the picture and hit me right in the gut.

That. That's the kind of relationship I want. I want someone to look at me the way Donnie and Roger are looking at each other, like there's no one else in the room, no one else in the entire freaking world. I want to feel that kind of love, the all-consuming kind that sweeps me up and carries me away, that makes me do all kinds of wild and unthinkable things.

Miles and I didn't have that. Not even close.

Donnie did and he lost it. All of my insides hurt merely imagining what it must've been like for him. Like what I went through yesterday, but a million trillion times worse? That's agony. That's unbearable. That's fucking heartbreaking.

I shudder and put a hand on the desk to steady myself. The blotter has letters embossed in gold on the corner.

From the desk of RA.

RA? Roger? I snatch my hand back. Is this Roger's office?

Everything makes more sense now. The ancient laptop, the yellowing birthday cards. The books on the shelves that don't look like anything a spin instructor would read. Not unless he was interested in how to influence people, how to motivate employees, how to be a good leader. They have to be Roger's books.

Almost four years, Donnie said. And he still wears his wedding ring, still has some of Roger's clothes, and from the look of the place, he hasn't touched this office in all that time. Now that I know to look for it, his grief is dripping off all the things in this room and the way they're immaculately maintained.

My insides hurt all the more. My guilt at being in the house doubles and triples and I stumble out of the room. I close the door firmly behind me.

Fuck. There was a reason the door was closed. There was a reason Donnie hadn't mentioned it when he'd told me about the theater room and home gym downstairs. Those, I'm welcome to. This, I'm not.

I back away from Roger's office, sending up a silent apology to wherever Roger is now. Maybe I should sequester myself in the guest room until Donnie gets home, just to be safe. Or like, as a punishment or something.

The bag of peas is getting a little mushy in my hand. If nothing else, I should stick it back into the freezer. I can bring my laptop down to the kitchen and try to do some work. There was that huge window down there that might be nice to sit next to.

I navigate carefully down the stairs, bag of peas in one hand, my laptop in the other. Between the bottom of the stairs and the kitchen is a living room with a comfy-looking sectional and a large gas fireplace. Then a formal dining room that has enough seating for ten. The kitchen is sleeker than I remember from yesterday. A big island runs down the middle, separating the cooking area from the casual dining table we sat at last night.

And the windows. Which are actually massive sliding doors that open onto a patio. There's a barbecue sitting in one corner and a set of stairs that lead down into a backyard. Holy shit, Donnie has a backyard. It's not huge and it's kinda messy with the last remnants of winter, but it's there. Whoa.

This house is no joke. Spin instructors don't make *that* much money, do they? Maybe Roger had a well-paying job. From the looks of his office, probably something in management, probably something important. Damn.

I hesitate while tossing the peas back into the freezer, not sure if Donnie really wants to eat them now that they've been on my foot. I put them in anyway. He can throw them out later if he wants. I settle at the table, facing the window and the bright sun that's shining through it. Donnie's left the WIFI password and his phone number on a slip of paper for me.

The second my computer connects to the internet messages start pouring in. *Ding, ding, ding.* They're syncing automatically from my phone and every last one of them is from Miles or Wyatt. I cover my face with my hands, but it's too late. I've already gotten a glimpse of them and they're all, "it's not what it looks like," and "we can explain."

"We." Like they're a unit and I'm the outsider. Like they're a team and I'm the one breaking them apart. I slump down in my chair and drop my head back to stare up at the ceiling. It takes forever for the fucking *ding-ing* to stop.

I squeeze my eyes shut. Okay, I can do this. I have to do this. The sooner I get it over with, the faster I can get on with… I don't know, the rest of my fucking life. My heart is in my throat and my hand trembles as I swipe my finger across the trackpad. I fist the fabric of the sweatpants just to have something to hold on to, like it can keep me from getting swept away by Miles and Wyatt's bullshit.

And it is all bullshit. The messages from this morning are more, "where are you," and "we're worried about you." Yeah, well, if they're so fucking worried about my well-being, maybe they should've kept their fucking dicks in their fucking pants.

There are a couple messages in the group chat with my cousins. Mostly memes that aren't really all that funny. And then there's one that makes me stop and curse.

WYATT

Check your email. They want to interview
us for the grant.

Jesus fucking Christ on a stick.

I pull up my inbox and find the email Wyatt forwarded to me. It's from a film production grant we applied for months ago. Thirty thousand dollars to young, queer filmmakers for a cutting-edge project. It was a long shot when we applied for it and I honestly didn't think we had a chance.

But here it is. An invitation to move on to the next phase of the application process. An interview with the granting committee to talk about our vision for the project and how it'll further queer filmmaking.

My jaw is on the floor. I want to cry except I don't know whether they're happy tears or sad tears. This is… huge, like fucking ginormous. I should be jumping up and down and shouting at the top of my lungs. This is as far as we've ever gotten with grants like this—it might be the furthest we ever get.

I push away from the table and pace over to the window.

The thing is, Wyatt's not just my best friend from film school. He's my creative partner too. We collaborated on almost every film project we had at school and we've been working together ever since graduation. I'm the creative genius. Wyatt's the business wiz. Together we were going to make quirky independent films and then take the world by storm.

But now…

Now, I don't know if I can stand being in the same room as him. I don't even want to see his fucking face. How am I supposed to go to an interview with him, put on a smile for film industry bigwigs, and pretend that everything's still hunky-dory? I can't. I just can't.

I bang my head against the window and the coolness of the glass sends shivers down my spine.

If this interview doesn't happen, there's no grant. No grant means no film. No film means I'm right back where I started—worse off than where I started. At least back then I had a creative partner, a dream, and a plan for how to get there. With Wyatt out of the picture, the dream starts getting hazy and the plan is null and void. Making films without Wyatt was never an option. I've never contemplated having a career where Wyatt wasn't an integral part.

This city is filled with wannabe filmmakers who think they're going to be the next Martin Scorsese or Stanley Kubrick or Francis Ford Coppola. Most of them never actually produce a film, they never see their names in the credits, they barely get close to a film set. Wyatt and I are supposed to be different. We're supposed to go places, do things, and become respected members of the industry.

This grant is supposed to be the first step.

I don't know what to do. It would be idiotic to throw away an opportunity like this and I don't *want* to throw it away. But I don't know how I'm going to keep working with Wyatt either. I can't trust him. How do I work on something so important with someone I don't trust?

I glare at my computer and the mess that waits for me on it. I can't deal with it right now. I need to get out of my own head.

The stairs leading down to the basement are between the kitchen and the dining room and it's calling out to me. The theater room is down there and Donnie said—explicitly—that I could use it. At the very least, I can check it out.

I close my laptop and take it with me downstairs. There's a small hallway with three open doors. A bathroom. A gym with a wall of mirrors, a treadmill, and a full set of weights, mats, and exercise balls. Then, the theater.

My jaw hangs open as I stare. The room is tiered like an actual movie theater, except instead of fold-down seats, there are plushy recliners and a couch. A projector is mounted to the ceiling and beside the door is an alcove in the wall with all the controls. This isn't some random dark room with chairs and a TV. This is a legit theater.

It doesn't take me long to get my computer hooked up

to the system and even less time for me to find the movie I want to watch.

Kill Bill Vol. 1. Uma Thurman and Lucy Liu in an all-out battle of blood and gore. It's the best revenge movie of all time and Quentin Tarantino at his best. It's exactly what I need.

DONNIE

I pull my earbuds out as I open the door to the house. It's quiet inside. "Connor?"

No answer. He's definitely home though. His coat is still hanging from the rack by the door. He isn't in the kitchen or in his bedroom upstairs. The only other option is in the basement—he better not be in the gym.

The door to the theater room is open and on the screen is the default "Ready to Cast" image of the projection system. Connor is curled up in one of the recliners. The armchair is fully extended, but he's folded his big body into a ball, one arm wrapped around his knees, the other hand tucked under his head. He's fast asleep.

I rushed out of Mars after my last class ended, dodging both Sawyer and Beau before they could stop me with questions I don't want to answer and frankly, don't have the answers to. That confrontation with Beau in the morning isn't like me. I don't get into arguments with people. I don't get angry over something that has almost nothing to do with me. There's something about Connor though, that's bringing out every single protective instinct I possess.

I don't usually rush out of Mars like I did either. Most days I linger and chat with gym members, answer their questions, and give them tips on exercise routines or healthy diets. If it's late, I'll stay to help Sawyer close up. I never really have anywhere else to be. I don't have anyone waiting for me in this big, empty house. But I do today, and the anticipation had me practically running home.

I quietly flick the switch to turn the projector off and the change in lighting makes Connor stir. He blinks and stretches before lifting his head and spotting me.

"Oh hey, you're home."

My heart skips a beat at those two words. *You're home.* They seep into me and warm me up until I feel all gooey and soft. There's someone waiting for me and they're happy that I'm finally here. My knees are weak, and I take a step toward the door before I sink right down into that recliner with Connor.

"How's your ankle?" I croak.

Connor rights the recliner and sticks his foot out to rotate his ankle around. "Good. The swelling's gone."

"Does it hurt to walk on it?"

He shakes his head with a yawn and reaches up to stretch. His shirt rides up, revealing a swath of skin at his waist and a line of dark blond hair that runs down into his jeans. I look away as the warmth in me heats up.

Now that my body's had a taste of what it's been missing for the past several years, it's hungry for all the touch it can get. It wants the hugs and the spooning, the sitting in laps and cuddling on the couch. It wants to feel the glide of skin against skin, the weight of another body pinning it to the bed, the stretch and burn of a cock sliding inside. It wants everything and the craving is so strong I can hardly breathe.

"I'll start cooking," I say, spinning toward the door and not waiting for Connor to follow.

Except he's right behind me. Close enough for me to feel the air stir as he moves. Close enough for his voice to slither down my spine.

"How was the gym?" he asks.

I busy myself with pulling out ingredients from the fridge, debating whether I should tell him about Miles showing up. The protective streak I've suddenly developed doesn't want to. It's better for him to make a clean break. But I'm not actually anyone to Connor and I don't have the right to be protective of him that way.

"Um, well, apparently Miles stopped by this morning." I try to keep my tone casual, no big deal, no need for Connor to find out about the whole thing with Beau.

Connor's quiet and when I look over at him, he's as still as a statue. His lips are pressed tightly together and the color's drained from his face. My stomach sinks and I wish there was another way—a better way—to do this.

"What did he want?"

"He was looking for you," I say quietly. "It was before I got there and Sawyer talked to him. He didn't tell Miles where you are though."

Connor's nod is jerky and his shoulders are halfway up to his ears. "What else?"

"That's it. When Sawyer said he didn't know where you were, he left."

Connor's eyes look unfocused and his chest isn't moving. Is he holding his breath?

"Connor?"

He starts and sucks in a lungful of air. "Yeah, what? Sorry."

Now that he's breathing again he's actually quivering a bit. I round the end of the island to where he's sitting on a stool and put my hand on his shoulder. "You weren't expecting him to show up at Mars, were you?"

Connor leans into my touch and the embers in me glow in delight. I slide my hand to his back and rub comforting circles across it.

"I'm surprised he even remembers the place. He hasn't used his membership in ages."

"But he knows you go regularly."

Connor shrugs and his shoulder brushes up against my stomach. I don't move away and neither does he.

"I guess."

"Have you spoken with him today?"

Connor shakes his head again and tilts it to the side so it rests against my chest. Any illusion that we're trying to keep our distance goes up in smoke. I hold him to me, my chin to my chest so his hair tickles my nose. The oxytocin pouring into my system makes everything kind of fuzzy and soft. Connor's warm against me, heavy against me, and when he loops his arm around my waist to fit us closer together, I nearly let out a moan. I don't know if I'm giving him comfort or if he's giving me comfort. Either way, it's astonishingly peaceful to hold him like that.

"They've been messaging me, but I haven't responded to anything," Connor says softly, his eyelashes fluttering closed.

"You don't have to if you don't want to."

A crease forms between his brows and his bottom lip sticks out. "I kinda do though."

He nuzzles my chest and it sparks a fire that travels through my limbs. It climbs to my head, making me dizzy with want, and pools in my groin, bathing my dick in heat. I shift to avoid poking Connor with my hard-on. He shifts too, pulling me closer.

This is so inappropriate. I shouldn't be holding him like this. I shouldn't even be touching him. Not if something as innocuous as his cheek on my chest is going to give me a raging boner. And especially not when he's sorting through the mess of a cheating boyfriend.

I tear myself out of his arms and feel utterly bereft when I'm out of touching range. It's ridiculous, how much I'm thirsting for him. Just being in the same room with his little pout and his thick body is driving me right to the edge. I haven't been this horny since puberty and it's more than embarrassing.

I pick up the chef's knife and start cutting the red pepper and broccoli—something, anything to keep my hands occupied so I don't reach for him again. "You can respond to them when you want to. Do it on your own terms, not on theirs."

Connor's hands are on the counter and he's twisting his fingers into a knot. "There's this grant that Wyatt and I applied for. They want to interview us as part of the application process. We need to respond and schedule a time for the interview."

I keep chopping, sneaking glances in Connor's direction when I'm not in danger of slicing through a finger. "What's the grant for?" I realize I don't even know what

Connor does for work or why he would need any kind of grant.

"Film production." His voice gets smaller and smaller as he speaks. "Wyatt and I met in film school and we've been trying to get this project off the ground for ages."

"You're a filmmaker." I would never have guessed that on my own, but now that Connor's said it, I can see it. There's a flair about him, something enigmatic that keeps drawing me in.

"A wannabe filmmaker. My day job is at a commercial production company. We make videos for companies. Training videos or event videos or promotional videos for websites. Sometimes actual commercials."

I switch out the chef's knife and cutting board to slice beef into bite-sized chunks. "Is that not filmmaking?"

Connor's mouth twists and he scrunches up his nose like he smells something rancid. "Not really? At least, that's not the type of thing I wanna make."

"And what would you rather be making?"

"Horror movies."

I don't hide my reaction very well. Connor takes one look at my face and snickers.

"You don't like horror movies?"

An icy shiver runs down my back. "Ew, no. Why would I want to watch something that scares the crap out of me?"

"Because it's fun."

I stare at him incredulously. Who knew cute-as-pie Connor would be into scary movies? "You like being scared?"

"Yeah." Connor's eyes are dancing and his smile is mischievous. "Especially when you're curled up on the couch and a cute guy hides his face behind your shoulder because he's too afraid to watch."

I see where he's going with this. "Right, and when the shoulder isn't enough, you suggest he hides his face in your crotch."

Connor's laugh hits me right where he was rubbing his face earlier. The middle of my chest tingles like I've been zapped and the sensation skitters across my skin. I want to wrap myself up in that laugh. I want to press my mouth to his and swallow it down.

"Now you're getting the idea." He smiles at me like I'm some kind of hero and I spin toward the stove to start heating up a pan.

"So, um, you'll have to work with Wyatt for the grant?" I ask, keeping my back to him. It's safer that way.

He doesn't answer right away and I peek over my shoulder at him. He's pouting again and it's my fault. I want to bring back that smile, that laugh.

"Sorry, we don't have to talk about that."

Connor sighs and his shoulders slump forward. "This grant is kind of a big deal and if there's any chance that we could get it, it feels stupid to throw it away. But I don't know if I can work with Wyatt anymore. I mean, what if we go through this whole process and don't get the grant in the end? Or what if we do get it and then I'll have to keep working with Wyatt for even longer!"

None of those options sound all that spectacular and I don't know what to tell him. Make up with Wyatt because no guy is worth throwing away something so important? Or cut his losses and apply for other grants on his own? It's a big decision and he's got a lot of emotion tainting his perspective right now. I know less than nothing about the film industry, so I have no clue what direction to point him in.

"Is there anyone you can talk to about this? Someone who knows the industry well?"

Connor blinks and furrows his brow. "Maybe Rick. He's my boss. There's a professor from school I keep in touch with."

"Maybe they can help you see the bigger picture."

Connor nods, his expression serious. "Yeah, that's a good idea. Thanks."

I didn't actually do anything, but I'll take the shy smile he sends my way. I hold it close and let it fuel the embers he's brought to life inside me.

CONNOR

"I cannot believe you've never seen *The Count of Monte Cristo*! Hello, Jim Caviezel? Guy Pearce? Baby Henry Cavill? With sideburns! In cravats!"

Donnie stares at me like I'm speaking a different language. "I don't know. Maybe? If I have seen it, I don't remember it. Must not have been memorable."

"Oh my god, sacrilege! This is an emergency. We need to remedy this."

We've finished our dinner of beef and broccoli on cauliflower rice, which—again—isn't bad, but isn't rice. Now we're in the middle of cleaning up and Donnie drops this bombshell on me. It isn't his first. He's never seen *Casablanca* or *Citizen Kane* or *Dr. Strangelove* either. Never mind *Psycho* or *Carrie* or *The Exorcist*. I'm sleeping under the same roof as a film virgin and I have my work cut out for me.

"It's not that I don't like movies. They just... don't make an impression, I guess."

I take the plate Donnie hands me and run the microfiber cloth over it until it's dry. "Okay, name one movie that's made an impression."

Donnie narrows his eyes as he thinks. "*Titanic?*"

"Oh my god!" I set the plate down carefully and snap the towel at Donnie.

He screeches and darts away, laughing. He looks amazing like that with his hazel eyes dancing and the laugh lines around his mouth and eyes out in full force. It's been like this for most of dinner. Jokes and teasing and easy conversation that flows like we've known each other forever.

It's comfortable. Not like old sneakers comfortable, where you should've replaced them ages ago, but couldn't be bothered. More like finding that perfect pair of jeans that you buy in every available color.

Being with Donnie feels so normal it's kinda freaky. We really have very little in common. He's all into healthy eating and staying active. He knows *a lot* about how the body works. None of that is surprising because obvs, he's Donnie, The Spin Instructor. But he also reads like, five books a week and listens to all kinds of weird music.

Movies and TV, though? Not so much. Not huge into Broadway either—musicals or plays. He almost never eats out and there are like, no snacks in the house. At least, nothing *I* would consider a snack. Granola is not a snack. At most, it's breakfast. I need chips.

Donnie and I stand off in the kitchen. Him with wet and soapy fingers. Me with my towel-snapping skills. We stalk around each other in circles, each waiting for the other to strike first.

"Connor," Donnie warns. There's a twinkle in his eyes that urges me on.

"Donnie." I mimic his tone, holding my towel in attack mode.

"What do you think you're doing?"

"What does it look like I'm doing?"

I take a step toward Donnie, and he takes a step back. I take another step forward, and he bumps into the wall. He's trapped and I smile like Jack Nicholson coming through the door in *The Shining*.

Except Donnie's faster than I give him credit for. Before I manage to pounce, he crouches and surges toward me, catching me around the middle. I stumble backward and tumble to the floor, bringing him with me. He lands on top of me with an *oomph*, and we both launch into a full-on tickle fight.

It isn't a fair competition at all. Donnie's not ticklish. I, on the other hand, I'm extremely ticklish. I squirm, trying to protect my sides. It feels like Donnie's evil-ass fingers are everywhere, all at once, and I can't fight him off fast enough. I can't breathe when I'm fighting for my life like this and my lungs burn until I feel like I'm going to pass out.

Donnie's totally the superior tickler. I'm a complete wuss. "Stahp! Please! I surrender!"

Donnie relents, finally, and I lay on the floor gasping for air. He's still on top of me, his chest rising and falling against mine. His one leg is between my thighs, pressed snugly against my groin—I might have accidentally trapped it there when I was flapping around like a dying fish.

Earlier, when he was giving me a hug, I'm pretty sure I

felt something against my thigh. Donnie shifted away and when I shifted back, it was there again. It was at the right height, the right shape, and the right firmness too. I'm feeling it again now, on my hip.

His lips hover an inch above mine. We're touching from shoulders to knees. His sweater is rucked up and my hands burn where they're in direct contact with his skin. Donnie's eyes darken as he gazes down at me and my dick responds, roaring to life.

I want to slide my palms under his sweater. I want to run my fingers along the valley of his spine. I want to angle my chin up and brush my lips over his. I want to tilt my hips and bring our erections together.

I lift my knee and Donnie gasps as my thigh nudges his cock. That sound. Holy shit, that sound. It's shaky and soft, like he's really sensitive, and it rips through me like a beast who's zeroed in on his prey.

My fingers tighten on his waist, holding him still as I grind my hips against his.

"Connor, fuck." Donnie breathes my name and drops his forehead to my shoulder. He exhales hot puffs of air onto my neck and I gasp at how delicate it feels.

I slide my hands down to cup Donnie's thick, muscled ass. He shudders violently in my arms.

"Oh god, wait. Wait, wait." He's on top of me for one more minute, sucking in a deep breath, then he's rolling off.

I let him go, even though it feels wrong.

He sits next to me, hunched forward, arms draped over his raised knees. His shoulders rise and fall as he breathes through whatever is going on in his head.

I stare at the ceiling, shivering now that I don't have Donnie to keep me warm.

It's only been twenty-four hours since I walked in on Miles and Wyatt. When I think about them, the rage and pain crash through me so hard it feels like I'm having some sort of panic attack. But when I don't think about them, when I'm with Donnie and we're laughing and smiling, I don't give a flying fuck what Miles and Wyatt did.

When I'm touching Donnie, all I want is to press up on him, get as close as possible to him, and crawl inside his skin. It's so comfortable there. It's so safe and warm. I want to tangle myself up with him and never let go.

He's still wearing his wedding ring. Roger's office is still sitting up there, untouched. I'm a random stray he's picked up off the side of the road. He doesn't need me humping him on the kitchen floor.

"I'm sorry," I say, sitting up.

Donnie starts, his shoulders shooting up to his ears. "I'm the one who should be sorry."

What does he have to be sorry for? He's been nothing but kind and generous and caring.

"Is your ankle okay?"

I rotate it to the left, then to the right. "It feels fine."

He nods and stands up. "Come on," he says, not looking at me. "Let's finish up the dishes."

I grab the towel from the floor and switch it out for a clean one. When I take the next plate from Donnie, our fingers brush and he sucks in a silent gasp.

I really hope I haven't crossed a line. It's not even about having a place to stay. I like Donnie. I'd like us to be friends, if we can. The last thing I want is for him to regret having invited me into his home.

DONNIE

We end up going down to the theater room after dinner for my so-called re-education. Connor has declared that my lack of film knowledge is unacceptable and he can't possibly share the same roof with someone who hasn't watched Alfred Hitchcock's entire filmography. I don't mention that I can't name a single Hitchcock film. There's one with birds, isn't there?

"Don't worry," Connor says, slowly navigating the stairs.

He says his ankle is fine, but I see him being cautious with it and it gives me a little buzzy feeling that he's listening to me.

"We'll start with something easy and work our way up to horror movies."

I'm behind him, carrying a big bowl of popcorn—salted *and* buttered for Connor's benefit—so he doesn't see the alarm on my face. I'm not a film buff by any stretch of the imagination, but I can enjoy a feel-good movie every once in a while, even some action ones too. I draw the line at horror films though. I'll have to find something to distract him before we get anywhere close to scary.

"Is this going to be one of those 'the book is better than the movie' situations?" I ask, hanging back to let Connor pick a spot.

He claims one side of the long couch and if I'm smart, I should go for a recliner on the far side of the room. I take the other side of the couch and set the bowl of popcorn between us. It'll have to do.

"No, it's not. The movie is fantastic." Connor's bent over his computer, fiddling with the trackpad.

I grab a few blankets from the basket in the corner and drop one at Connor's feet. "Have you read *The Count of Monte Cristo*?"

Connor's eyes dart in my direction, then back to his computer. "It's a long book, okay? I'm more of a moving pictures kinda guy. Have *you* read the book?"

I scoff and put on my best Queen's English. "Of course I have. In university."

"Show off." Connor smirks as he spreads his blanket across his lap. His feet are tucked up under him and he slides down until his head rests against the back of the couch.

The film flickers to life on the screen in front of us and beside me, Connor keeps up a steady crunch of popcorn. He's so engrossed already, eyes glued to the screen even though it's still only the opening credits.

Earlier, on the kitchen floor, it was a miracle I managed to roll off him. When he shoved his thigh between my legs, when he ground himself against me... even now, I'm getting hard remembering it. He wanted to kiss me. I saw it in his eyes. I felt it in the way his hands tightened on my waist, the way his lips parted and his body molded to mine.

This attraction isn't one-sided anymore. That doesn't mean it's a good idea to act on it. Connor isn't the least bit over what happened with Miles and Wyatt, and anything that happens now is only going to be a knee-jerk emotional reaction. It'll be revenge, a rebound. I don't want him to do something he's going to regret later. I don't want to be the thing he regrets.

Connor shifts on the couch and his knee bumps the bowl of popcorn. I catch it before it goes tumbling to the floor. It's almost empty now and I should set it aside so it's out of the way, but I keep it between us. It's a flimsy reminder that I need to keep my distance.

He stretches and folds his arm behind his head. We're close enough that if I turn toward him, I'll be staring straight into his armpit. The scent of body wash wafts over me, warm and spicy, making me want to lean in a little closer. I want to run my nose across the soft skin of his neck. I want to lick the strong line of his collarbone.

I need to resist temptation and remember why he's in my house in the first place. Connor is off-limits. It doesn't matter how much my body craves his touch. It doesn't matter how much he might be attracted to me in return. Neither of us is in a place where we can make rational, informed decisions.

Connor isn't watching the screen anymore. He's watching me. The side of my face heats with the weight of his gaze and I can't not turn to meet it. Under the flickering lights of the movie, his eyes are dark and there's no mistaking the want radiating off him. It would be so easy.

Just a few inches from my side and a few inches from his and I'll know what those lips feel like on mine. My breath hitches in my chest. My fingers curl into the blanket on my lap so I don't reach for him.

The longer he stares at me and the longer I stare back, the more difficult it is to list all the reasons why we shouldn't do this. Connor takes the bowl between us and I don't stop him when he moves it off to the side. He extends his arm across the back of the couch, and when it brushes against my hair, I slide down until I'm on my side, head on his thigh. He rearranges my blanket for me, making sure I'm covered from neck to feet. Then he rests his arm so it's draped along my body, hand on my stomach.

I can't breathe. Every inhale brings in more of his clean, alluring scent. Every exhale settles his arm more heavily on my side. My lungs burn with the need for oxygen and when I finally succumb, I'm done. He's all around me and it feels so goddamn good. It's too much. I can't resist it. I don't really want to.

My eyes drift shut as I sink into him and let him envelop me. Just for a little bit, just for tonight. This isn't any more than what we've done already. It doesn't mean anything. It's *fine*.

I drift in and out of semi-consciousness while the Count of Monte Cristo doles out his revenge, and when I finally open my eyes again, the screen is black and the credits are rolling. Connor's fingers are combing through my hair and oh god, my dick is hard and my balls are tight and fuck, I want him so much.

I force myself to sit up and every cell in my body protests. I force myself to stand and my legs are on the verge of revolting. I busy myself with folding up the blanket, keeping my eyes pointed anywhere but at him.

Connor powers down the system and turns off the lights. We climb the stairs in silence. The air is heavy and thick with our mutual desire. I have to actively measure the distance between us to make sure I don't unconsciously drift closer to him.

In the kitchen, I fill a glass with water and hand it to him. His fingers brush mine and a spark zings straight through me, landing in my groin. I gasp. Connor's gaze shoots to my face. I pull my hand away and it's unsteady as I fill a second glass for myself.

He follows me up to the second floor and I pause before turning to go up to my room on the third. Connor's standing too close. I can feel the heat of his body through our clothes. He doesn't go into his room, and when I lift my gaze to his, I can see my own mess of emotions reflected in his eyes. Common sense battles with overwhelming desire and it's a toss-up which one will come out on top. I have a sinking feeling that lust is going to win.

"Goodnight," I force myself to say.

Connor leans an inch away from me. Instead of making it easier to breathe, there's an invisible tether tugging me toward him. I grip the banister to keep myself from following him into his room.

"I, um, need to go get my things from the apartment tomorrow," Connor says, looking off to the side. "Is it okay if I bring stuff back here?"

"Of course. Do you…" This is probably a bad idea. "…need help?"

Connor's gaze snaps back to mine and the hope in his eyes is staggering.

"I can come with you if you'd like." To pack, to carry boxes, or you know, because I can't stand the idea of Connor having to go back there by himself. Even if it means getting closer to him when I should be maintaining my distance. Even if it means wading deeper into the emotional and sexual quagmire when I should be trying to get out.

"Yeah? I'm not like, derailing your plans for tomorrow or anything?"

If I had plans for tomorrow, they're canceled now. There's no way I can say no to Connor when he looks at me like that, big doe eyes brimming with anxiety. Helping him get through this next hurdle is more important than my need for self-preservation.

"No plans, I'm all yours for the day." I tack on the last three words quickly, because saying that I'm Connor's, whew, that's stirring something inside me that I don't want to examine too closely.

"Thank you," Connor says shyly. He goes to his room and pauses in the doorway. We stare at each other for a moment and a wordless message passes between us. Something's happening here, something that neither of us expected. Something that we might not have any control over.

I force myself to turn away from him and climb up the stairs. His door snicks shut behind me and I let out a big sigh of... not quite relief, not even resignation, more like an acknowledgment that Connor isn't merely a temporary house guest. His being here is changing me and the way I've been living for the past four years.

I'm not sure I like it, but I'm not sure I have a choice. I've been in a kind of holding pattern since Roger died, somewhere between an unmitigated disaster and thriving. I've been functional and it's been enough. I've gotten used to it and I'm not looking for anything more. Life doesn't always give me what I want though.

I mindlessly change into pajamas, brush my teeth, and slap some skin products on my face. I climb into bed with my reading glasses and eReader. The words blur together and float around on the screen. After a few minutes, I set it aside, take my glasses off, and turn off the light.

The bed is still big. The sheets are still cold. It hasn't bothered me in a while, but I can't help dwelling on it now. It was so nice to lie on the couch with Connor, to feel the warmth of someone beside me, to hear the steady inhale and exhale of his breathing. My body misses that feeling, it aches for it.

I hug a pillow to my chest and try to imagine that it's Roger. But as I drift off to sleep, I'm not entirely sure it's still Roger I have in my mind.

CONNOR

We're standing across the street from my apartment. My *old* apartment. The building is familiar, the street is familiar, but I'm seeing it all through new eyes. It used to make me smile to be here, to be coming home to my boyfriend and the life we've built together. I used to feel so damn special. Not everyone gets to share an apartment with their boyfriend and build a fabulous career as a filmmaker with their best friend. I had it all. I had it made.

And now… now, if I never set foot on this fucking street again, it'll be too soon.

"Are you okay?" Donnie asks. "We don't have to do this today if you don't want to."

We do though. Unless I want to keep borrowing Roger's clothes, which would be fine, if I have to. But like, I'd like my own, if I can.

Also, I don't entirely trust Miles with all my things. It's not that he's going to do anything drastic like burn my collection of Blu-Rays or anything like that. I just don't like the idea of him and Wyatt having unfettered access to *my* stuff. It's mine. They can't have it.

It's going to be a quick in and out. I've timed it so that Miles should be at work so there's no risk of running into him. We've got extra-strength trash bags to throw everything into and once it's done, I never have to come back.

I want to grab Donnie's hand as we cross the street. I need the calmness he exudes, the way he anchors me with nothing more than a touch. My stomach is all twisted up in knots, and every little sound, every sudden movement at the corner of my vision makes me jump.

His hand comes to my back as I unlock the door to the building. It's a gentle pressure, barely there, but it's everything. My lungs expand and my heart stops trying to leap out of my throat. I want to collapse into his arms, but I can't—we need to do this thing.

The building is quiet when I let us in. "It's on the third floor."

We climb in silence. The only sounds are the *thump* of our footsteps and the jangle of keys in my hand. My ankle doesn't hurt anymore, but I'm still careful with it anyway.

At the door to the apartment, I slide the key into the lock and pause. Deep breath. No one is inside. Nothing bad is going to happen. Donnie's hand is on my back again.

"You've got this."

With him, I feel like I do.

I turn the key and open the door. The apartment is empty and I let out the breath I was holding. Thank-fucking-god.

It's messy. Dirty dishes sit on the kitchen counter. Dirty cups sit on the coffee table. Clothes are strewn all over the freaking place—on the couch, on the floor, on the unmade bed. I itch to start cleaning it all up.

No. I curl my fingers into fists. This isn't my mess, this isn't my apartment, and it's not my responsibility to pick up after Miles anymore. He can fucking pick up after himself. Better yet, get Wyatt to do it.

The rush of righteous anger is exactly what I need to get my ass into gear. "Let's start in the bedroom." I march in there and bite back my annoyance at the mess—*ignore it, it's not my problem.*

Donnie pulls out a trash bag and holds it open for me as I go through the closet. Pants and shirts from the hangers, the three suits I own. Sweaters from the shelf above and shoes on the floor. T-shirts and shorts are in the dresser, along with underwear and socks. The laundry basket is overflowing and it takes me a few minutes to sort Miles's shit from my own.

Thank god Donnie's here with me. Even if I didn't need the moral support—which I do—there's no way I can carry all this stuff out by myself.

Linens. I bought most of them, so I should take most of them, right? They're not super fancy, and I'm not super attached to them, but it's the principle of the matter. The nicest set is currently on the bed though, and do I want the hassle of stripping it? On the other hand, it'd be a very satisfying fuck-you if Miles comes home to a naked mattress. Yeah, I'm that kind of bitch.

I round the bed and something on the nightstand catches my eye. It's a mouthguard container. Not mine. Not Miles's. Neither one of us uses one. But Wyatt does.

I step back from the bed, pulling my hands away like the thing is going to open up and bite me. If Wyatt's keeping his mouthguard here, that means he's sleeping here. *Still* sleeping here. On my nicest set of bedsheets.

I don't want them anymore. I don't want any of them anymore. They're all contaminated now and I'd rather wash myself with bleach than touch them again. I'll buy new fucking linens. Higher thread count ones. Miles and Wyatt can eat shit.

Donnie comes back from hauling another full trash bag to the growing pile by the front door. "You all right?"

I spin away from the bed, jaw set and rage roiling inside me. "Yeah, fine. We're done in here."

That's when a key slides into the lock on the front door. I freeze. Blood rushes past my ears. My stomach drops past the soles of my feet.

Donnie's right there, standing in front of me, facing the bedroom doorway, one arm extended back to hold me close. My hands go to his back, searching for something to grab on to. They sink into the extra material around the waist of Donnie's coat.

"It's okay. You'll be okay," Donnie whispers over his shoulder at me. He seems taller all of a sudden, or maybe it's me who's cowering behind him. He's vibrating with an energy that makes me feel safe and protected even when I'm legit freaking out. He's right—I'll be okay, because he'll make sure that I am.

Miles takes his sweet-ass time, dropping his bag on the floor and some other stuff on the kitchen counter. It doesn't sound like he's noticed the trash bags he's walking right past. He's head down, bent over his phone, as he comes through the living room toward the bedroom. He only sees us when he's at the door.

He screams, drops his phone, and jumps, hitting the

wall behind him. "Holy fuck! Jesus Christ! What the hell are you doing here?" he yells, clinging to the door frame.

The fear, the anxiety, the panic of having to see Miles again, all of it evaporates into pure, unadulterated fury. I push past Donnie and get right up into Miles's face.

"This is still my apartment, asshole. My name is on the fucking lease. I can be here if I want to be here. What the fuck are *you* doing here? Aren't you supposed to be at work?"

Miles stands up straight, tugs on the hem of his shirt, and lifts his chin. "I called in sick."

If I could murder someone with my eyes… "You don't look sick to me."

"It's been… a difficult few days." Miles deflates a little, like *he's* the one who walked in on his boyfriend fucking his best friend. Like *he's* the one who's had his dreams shattered. Like *he's* the one who has to figure out how to put his life back together.

I want to wrap my hands around his puny little neck. "Are you fucking kidding me?" I roar. *I'm* the victim here. *I'm* the one they hurt. How dare Miles use my pain as an excuse to take time off? How very dare. He has no fucking right.

"Connor…" Whatever Miles is about to say dies on his lips when he notices Donnie coming up to stand beside me.

Donnie's hand settles on my back, heavy and solid, and it brings me back down to earth.

"Who are—wait, I know you from somewhere." Miles tilts his head to the side as he studies Donnie.

"Mars Fitness," Donnie says, wedging himself between me and Miles and pushing me back with his body. His voice is flat and hard and I crumple against him a little.

Recognition lights up Miles's eyes. "Oh yeah, the spin instructor. You're the one Connor talks about all the time."

I did *not* talk to Miles about Donnie all the time. Or maybe I did, but that's completely not the point right now.

Miles's brows slam together. "What are *you* doing here?"

Donnie doesn't miss a beat. "I'm helping Connor get his things. He's staying with me."

Miles's gaze drops to the half-filled trash bag at our feet, like he's only now figuring out what we're doing there. He looks between me and Donnie, at how close we're standing to each other, and his expression turns ugly.

"You're staying with *him*? Why the hell would you do that?"

I try to lunge at him, but Donnie's a rock and he doesn't budge. I rise onto my toes and shout over his shoulder instead. "It's none of your goddamn business who I stay with. What, did you think I was sleeping on the fucking street this whole time?"

Miles blanches and drops his gaze to the floor. That's fucking right. Be ashamed. Be very ashamed.

I drop back on my heels and suddenly the room is spinning. I grasp at Donnie to keep from falling over. His arm comes around me to hold me up and he slips the other hand between the unzipped front of my coat to flatten his palm on my chest.

"Breathe," he orders.

I suck in a breath.

"That's it. Again."

I take another. The spinning room slows and finally stops. My heart is still pounding and my hands tingle with numbness. Donnie's supporting most of my weight. My eyes prickle with tears I don't want to shed and I desperately need to lie down and curl into a ball. I want Donnie to take me away from here. I want him to take me home—his home—and hold me until the world makes sense again.

"Are you fucking him?"

The words pierce through me like a blade in my gut. Donnie goes frighteningly still. He pushes me behind him and rounds on Miles who shrinks back against the wall.

"So what if we are? What is it to you?" He's growling. He's menacing. I would never have imagined sweet, caring Donnie could be so dark and threatening. It sends chills down my spine and I'm not even the one he's speaking to.

Miles either has balls of steel or zero sense of self-preservation. I'm voting for the latter. "It's a little fast, don't you think? In my bed one night and in yours the next?"

What on god's green planet did I ever see in Miles? Has he always been like this and I was dating some fantasy person I made up in my mind? Because the guy I knew wouldn't be like this. But then, I guy I knew wouldn't have cheated on me either. So I guess I never really knew Miles at all.

DONNIE

Miles is cowering in front of me, but there's this arrogant obstinance in his stare. In other circumstances, I would be impressed. If we were in my spin room, I might even be proud. Right now, I'm furious.

This bitch thinks he can sleep around on Connor and then accuse him of being a slut? Not if I have anything to say about it. "That's rich, coming from you. Exactly how many times have you dropped your pants and bent over for Wyatt's cock?"

Miles's face turns so red it looks like steam is going to come out of his ears and the top of his head is going to pop off. "That's not the same thing."

I sneer at him and give him a disgusted once-over. "You've got that right."

Miles looks primed for a fight, and as satisfying as it would be to sink my fist into his face, I take several steps away from him, pushing Connor back as I go. This is quickly spiraling out of control and I don't quite recognize myself in the middle of it all. I'm not a violent person. I've never thrown a punch in my entire life. I'm not about to throw away that track record on Miles of all people.

"Maybe you should step outside until we finish up," I say to Miles. It isn't a suggestion.

Miles swallows visibly and exits to the living room.

I turn to Connor and he's immediately in my arms, face buried under the collar of my coat, cheek against my neck. His body chemistry is completely out of whack and he's shaking so hard, he's either going to bounce off the walls or cave in on himself. I rub my hands up and down his back and whisper all the soothing words.

"Shh, it's okay, darling. I've got you. Everything's going to be fine." It takes way too long for him to come back to himself. He's not going to be able to stay on his feet for much longer. I need to get him out of here. Now. "Do you think you can get the rest of your things?"

Connor pulls away but he keeps his hands on my chest like he needs them there to steady himself. I grip his arms, ready to catch him if his knees go out from under him.

He nods. "I think so."

"Let's move quickly, okay? Just the most important things, the sentimental things you can't live without. Everything else is replaceable."

He meets my eyes and I pour as much of my strength and resilience and determination into him as I can. I need him to hold it together for a little bit longer, then he can break into as many pieces as he wants.

We tie up the last of the trash bags in the bedroom and drag them out to the living room. Miles, the bastard, is still there, leaning against the far wall, staring daggers at us. We ignore him.

I shake out a new bag and Connor starts handing me books from the bookcase. Some of them look like textbooks from school. There are a couple coffee table books about different eras of the film industry. He's got an impressive stack of Blu-Rays, but apparently, no machine to watch them with.

He grabs the antique-looking quilt off the back of the couch and the hoodie hanging over the arm.

"Wait, that's Wyatt's." Miles pushes himself off the wall, eyes glued to the hoodie.

Connor holds it up. It's got a seal across the front with the name of Connor's film school underneath. "This? No, it's mine. Wyatt's hoodie has a zipper, mine doesn't." His voice drips with venom and it fills me with raw satisfaction.

I take the hoodie from him and stuff it into a bag.

"He's waiting to hear from you, you know," Miles says, a little softer now, a little less confrontational.

Connor flinches and I take his arm to tug him away from Miles. Whatever Miles is talking about, it can wait. "Anything else in here?"

He shakes his head and goes into the bathroom. I stand in the doorway and glare at Miles. He glares back.

There are silly selfies stuck to the front of the fridge and a corny sombrero on the wall. The TV looks moderately expensive and so does the sound system attached to it. Connor probably set that up, knowing what I do now about his love for films. Those'll be a bitch to lug out of here if Connor wants to take them though. I'm not sure it's worth it, especially since we've already got the theater room at home.

Mine and Connor's home. Together. It feels right

thinking about it like that. Like he's lived there for longer than two nights, like it's always been ours.

My initial offer to him was for as long as he needed to get back on his feet, but there's no reason why he can't stay indefinitely. I've said it before, I'm not using that space for anything else and frankly, it's kind of nice having another person in the house. It's nice having someone to come home to, someone to spend the evenings with, someone to cook for and eat meals with. I like having Connor around. Maybe he likes it too.

I push the thought aside, along with the fizzy excitement of something new on the horizon. There's still the issue of Connor grieving his relationship with Miles and the question of what he's going to do about working with Wyatt in the future. I'm still carrying around a shite ton of baggage myself. Whatever could happen and whatever should happen are conversations for another day.

Connor pours the last of the bathroom stuff into a bag and then squeezes past me to go to the kitchen. He pulls down a few novelty mugs from a cabinet and I find a bag with clothes to wrap them up.

"Anything else?" I ask, tying the bag shut.

He scans the space. What does he see when he looks at it now? A past that he's eager to leave behind? Or something precious that he's lost? Maybe a little bit of both.

He shakes his head, eyes on Miles. "No, there's nothing else worth taking."

It's going to take us several trips to move all the bags. I send Connor downstairs to handle the second leg, while I bring the bags from the apartment out to him. We end up filling an entire UberXL, leaving just enough space to wedge ourselves into the backseat.

I sit flush against the door on one side and Connor is practically on my lap on the other. As the car pulls away from the curb, I lift my arm over Connor's head and he curls himself into me.

"It's over. It's done," I whisper to him while holding his head to my shoulder.

He's sniffling, he's shaking, he's crashing harder than he did that first night I brought him home.

Our driver peers at us through the rearview mirror. "He okay?"

I nod. "Yeah, he'll be fine." My voice isn't nearly as steady as I thought it was going to be. I'm crashing too.

The driver shoots me a sympathetic look and follows his phone's directions to turn left. When we get back to the house, I almost ask the driver to go around the block a few more times. Connor's nowhere near ready for multiple trips back and forth to unload the car. I'd be surprised if he can stand up straight.

The driver puts the car into park. "You need a hand?"

Relief floods through me. "Yes, please, if you don't mind."

"No problem."

I half lead, half carry Connor up the stoop and deposit him on a couch in the living room. Then I run back out to where the driver is stacking our bags on the sidewalk.

"Thank you so much."

"Yeah, not a problem. He looks like he's having a rough go."

"It's definitely not his day."

We manage to get everything inside, dumped into piles that I'm going to have to climb over. But it's done.

"Have a good one." The driver waves to me and climbs back into the car.

I pull out my phone and make sure he gets a fucking massive tip.

Connor's lying on the couch, curled up on his side, and staring blankly into the middle of the room. I crouch down in front of him, putting my hand on his arm.

"Hey, how about we get you upstairs to bed." I watch his pupils dilate as he focuses on my face.

"Will you stay with me?"

God, yes, I'll stay with him. Not even for him. I need it for me. "Come on."

We climb the stairs like we're moving through molasses. Every step is a struggle, every step brings us closer to victory, and we only have each other to cling to along the way. We fall into Connor's bed like we're drowning men washed up on shore. I have barely enough energy to get us under the covers.

I drag Connor to me and he molds himself to my side, head on my shoulder, one leg tossed over my thighs. We sink into the mattress together. Home. Finally.

He's out almost immediately, but I stare at the ceiling for a while.

I don't recognize the man I became during that confrontation with Miles. He felt eerily like the man who had confronted Beau. Connor brings out something in me that I've never experienced before and frankly, it's kind of scary. I'm in my forties. I shouldn't be uncovering latent parts of my personality at this age, should I?

I mean, I've always been a caretaker, I've always been pretty protective of people who are important to me. But the way I stood up to Beau and the way I was actively trying to intimidate Miles, this is a whole other level entirely. This is like… maybe a little unhealthy.

The scariest part is, I would do it again. Both times.

My thumb drifts to my ring finger and I twirl the band around and around. If Connor had stumbled into Mars when Roger was still alive, Roger would've been just as furious at Miles as I was. He would've been just as frustrated with Beau too. I'm sure of it.

He would've let Connor stay in the guest room for as long as he needed to. But would he have invited Connor to move in with us? Probably not.

Except Roger's not here anymore. That old familiar surge of pain in my chest makes me gasp. He's not here and he's not coming back. I haven't been able to let go of him in all this time. Maybe this is the universe's way of forcing me to move on. Maybe Roger's out there somewhere, pushing Connor into my path, saying enough is enough.

I close my eyes against the tears that well up and spill over. I hold Connor tighter to me and he sighs in his sleep. I don't want to let go. I don't want to move on. I'm okay where I am.

But Connor's body feels breathtakingly good against mine. His smile fills me with warmth and his laugh makes me all giddy. I've been happier in the last two days than I've been in ages, even with the emotional rollercoaster we're riding.

I want him. And that's terrifying.

CONNOR

I'm running through a forest full of lemons. It doesn't make sense and I don't care. I just breathe in deeply and then drop to the ground to tumble around in some lemon-scented leaves. They smell so good, so soothing and comforting, and I burrow in deeper until I'm covered in them.

"Connor."

A deliciously husky, British voice whispers my name in my ear.

"Connor."

He sounds like he smiling, like he's trying not to laugh. But I want him to laugh, loud and bright, and I want to laugh with him until we're both exhausted and out of breath.

"Wake up, darling."

Wait a minute. I open my eyes to a dimly lit room and immediately slam them shut again. I want to go back to the lemon forest. I want to take Donnie with me. Then I'll never have to deal with the literal mountain of trash sitting downstairs and I'll never have to decide how I'm going to self-sabotage my career.

I groan and snuggle down into Donnie. I've been using him as a human pillow and I'm not sorry. He smells amazing, his body is the epitome of solid masculine beauty, and there's that notable erection against my thigh again.

I grind myself against him. Shameless, I know. He gasps and the hand he's got on my thigh grips me like he wants to crush me to him. I grind against him again.

"Connor," Donnie breathes. There is a hint of warning in it, but his arms are so tight around me, I'm not sure I could get out of his embrace even if I wanted to.

"Do you want me to stop?" I ask, whispering against that spot between his jaw and his ear.

Donnie shudders and for a split second, I'm afraid he's going to say yes.

"No, don't stop." He sounds tortured. His cock is a big, hard bulge against my leg.

I shift so I'm on my elbow above him, looking down at him. His eyes are dark with pure lust, his lips are parted, and when he lets out a tiny, desperate sound, that's all the permission I need.

I fit my mouth over his and holy fucking shit, my entire body springs to life. His tongue sweeps over mine and I feel the lick straight to the bottoms of my feet. My dick throbs painfully against the zipper of my jeans. My nipples ache where they brush against my shirt. Every inch of my skin is primed and I only need a single touch to burst into flames.

I slide my hands under Donnie's sweater and push them up his sides, taking his clothes with him. He sits up just long enough for me to pull it off him. I reach behind my head, grab the fabric at the nape of my neck, and tug my shirt off in one go.

Donnie shudders and grabs my face. "Fuck, I love it when you do that."

Do what? Take my shirt off? I'll do it for him every day if he wants.

His tongue is in my mouth again and his bare chest is a hard, rippled plain. He arches up and the glide of skin against hot skin burns through me. Christ, he feels so good. I press him down with my bulk and he whines, needy and hungry, and I drink up every single drop.

I want to make him come. I want to make him fall apart with pleasure. I want to milk every single sound he has inside him from the smallest whimper to the loudest scream, and once I've cataloged all of them, I want to do it again.

I drag my mouth away from his to taste the rest of him. His jaw, his neck, his collarbone, the dip at the base of his throat. There's a spot that's particularly tasty, right where his pulse beats strong and steady against my tongue. I seal my lips around it and suck. Donnie's voice rises an octave. *Yeeesss, give me more of that, baby.*

I lick my way down to his dusty brown nipples, nipping each with my teeth, then soothing them with my tongue. Donnie's fingers are in my hair, holding me to him, and I nip and sooth for as long as he needs.

When he lets me move on, I trace every ridge of his flat stomach with my fingers, then my lips, then my tongue, until his muscles are quivering like he's been holding a crunch for too long. Maybe he is. His entire body is taut, ready to snap at the slightest trigger. I want to have him in my mouth when it happens, I want to swallow him down when he explodes.

I curl my fingers under the waistband of Donnie's sweats and pull them down around his thighs. His cock is a hard length, trapped against the crease of his hip by the black fabric of his briefs. There's a wet spot at the tip and I suck it into my mouth.

"Oh, fuck," Donnie cries above me and I suck harder.

His pre-cum tastes delicious. I can only imagine how much better his actual cum will taste. I bury my nose down by his balls, under his balls, and breathe in his hot, musky smell. It makes my head spin and my dick pulse and I rub my face all over his groin.

His nails scrape over my scalp. His fingers tug at my hair. He rolls his hips as he shoves my head deeper. It feels like he's marking me with his scent and I am here for it.

I glance up at him. His eyes are half-lidded and his mouth is bruised from our kisses. He's staring down at me like I'm a miracle unfolding before his very eyes.

"God, you're gorgeous."

The words hit me deep. I've never been called gorgeous before. Cute, sure. Hot, sometimes. But gorgeous? Never. Not until Donnie.

"*You're* gorgeous," I say and Donnie's face flushes a pretty pink.

He didn't mean to say that out loud and somehow, that makes it all even more precious. I press a kiss to the flat of his stomach, taking the moment to soak in the feeling of him against my cheek. Then I hook my fingers over his briefs and push them down to join his sweats.

"So gorgeous," I say again. I run my lips from the base

of Donnie's cock, right to the tip, then wrap my lips around the head and suck.

"Oh, god!" Donnie's hips come off the bed and his cock slips deeper past my lips. I push him back down with my weight and follow him with my mouth until he's lodged in as far as he can go.

I've never come just from giving a blowjob before, though with Donnie's dick in my mouth, I might this time. It's perfectly thick and heavy on my tongue. It stretches my jaw the perfect amount. Donnie's fingers rake through my hair, igniting every single nerve ending in my body.

I moan at how good it is, and his balls pull tight in my palm. I roll them and squeeze them. I drag my other hand up Donnie's body and spread my fingers over the smooth muscles of his chest. Donnie tangles his fingers with mine and suddenly, this isn't merely a blowjob anymore.

This is… I don't know, deeper, more intimate, almost spiritual. We both need this so much, the physical connection, the emotional release. Donnie appeared in my life right when I needed him most and I would be lost without him. He's been my anchor over the past couple days, keeping me safe and secure when everything else is spinning out of control. I owe him so much more than I can put into words. Whatever he needs from me, whatever he wants, I'm going to give it to him.

"Connor! Connor!" Donnie's fingers grip mine so hard it feels like they're going to break. His nails might be drawing blood from my scalp.

I suck him deeper, harder. His balls draw up into his body and he's coming on my tongue. I throw my whole weight on him as he bucks and bends under me. I try to keep my mouth sealed around his cock to catch every drop of his cum, but some still leak out. His orgasm goes on forever and my mouth fills with the salty bitterness of his taste. It's a drug and I think I'm addicted.

Donnie's limp by the time he pumps out the last bit of cum onto my tongue. What I haven't already swallowed down, I lick up, making sure he's nice and clean. I tug his sweats and underwear down the rest of the way and toss them to the side.

As I climb back up his unbelievably sexy body, I stop at the V at his hips. It should be illegal for anyone to have hips this sexy. I run my tongue up one side and down the other and would have stayed to worship it more, except Donnie tugs at my shoulder.

Donnie attacks my mouth the second I get up there, shoving his tongue between my lips like he wants me to suck on it too. My dick hurts where it's still trapped in my jeans and Donnie's hand fondling it isn't helping. I moan and push my hard-on into his palm.

"Shh," Donnie whispers and flips us around so fast it makes me dizzy. "My turn now."

I lay on my back, shivering at the promise in his voice. He finds my nipples and pinches and twists them at the same time, the stinging pain shooting straight to my pulsing dick. He scrapes his blunt nails down my chest, my stomach, leaving trails of fire in their wake.

He trails them back up my sides, right over the spots where he knows I'm ticklish. I squawk and squirm, grabbing at his hands. He smirks at me, the fucker, and twines our fingers together. Palm to palm, he lifts them above my head and pins them there.

I still have my jeans on. I'm not particularly self-conscious about being naked around other guys. Yet, there's something about lying there with my arms above my head that leaves me exposed, opened up, and on display for him. I shudder at how vulnerable I am, at how good it feels to be vulnerable with Donnie. I've never felt like this with anyone else before and it's turning me on more than I've ever been in my whole life.

He kisses the inside of my arm, near my elbow, then again, a little lower. I'm so sensitive there, the skin is so tender, and the softness of his lips combined with the roughness of his stubble stirs up sensations that are blowing my mind. He keeps going, inching closer and closer to my armpit. The closer he gets, the less I can breathe. My eyes are glued to his mouth. He isn't going to do it. No way.

He flicks his gaze to me and pierces me with the intensity of his stare. Then he parts his lips, reaches his tongue out, and licks a long, wet stripe from the bottom of my armpit straight through to the top.

"Fuck!" A thrill runs through me like there's a horror movie playing out before me. I can't watch. I can't tear my eyes away. I need to know what happens next and I'm terrified of it at the same time.

Donnie latches onto a soft spot and sucks.

"Fucking Christ!" I yell. His mouth is on my armpit, but it feels like it's on my cock. Hot and wet and the suction is so goddamn intense. I honestly can't tell which is which. My hips jerk to get more. My arms strain against Donnie's hold. My underwear is so wet, I might actually have come already.

"Good?" Donnie asks, breath hot, lips tickling the hairs. His smile is pure fucking evil, like he's just put a spin class through its paces.

"Ahhh…" I moan weakly.

Donnie switches to my other arm and I swear to god, I almost die. His tongue swirls through the hairs and his teeth nip at the skin underneath. I'm struggling against him, desperate and afraid, and totally strung the fuck out.

"Donnie, please," I beg. "Please, I need to come."

He pauses and considers me for a second. If he goes back to my armpits, then I might as well expire right there because there's no way my body can handle any more. But he takes pity on me.

His lips are shiny with spit and the entire bottom half of his face is wet with it. He smiles like the devil as he palms my cock through my jeans. "You need to come?"

"Please." I grind my dick into his hand. I'll do anything to come. Anything.

Donnie starts undoing my jeans and holy fucking shit, it's almost worse. He's moving so slowly, gently squeezing the button out of its hole, dragging the zipper down one tooth at a time. He peels back the two sides and traces his finger along the length of my cock, barely touching it.

"Donnie!" I jerk my hips, chasing his finger.

"Shh," he whispers, leaning up to give me another kiss. It's wet and I eat it up, showing him how hungry I am for him, how needy I am. Tears—actual, honest-to-god tears—run out of the sides of my eyes and into my ears. That's how much I need to come.

Donnie shoves my underwear down and my cock springs out. His fingers curl into a tight, excruciating vise. It hurts so good. It's so deliciously painful. I've leaked so much pre-cum there's no need for lube. A couple pumps of Donnie's hand is all I need to empty my balls onto my stomach.

DONNIE

"Let's get those legs pumping! Come on, find the beat. Match my pace."

Every last bike is taken and the room is full of men bent over their handlebars, determination on their faces, all pedaling with the same rhythm. It makes the air vibrate with an energy that always gets my adrenaline going.

"Turn up your resistance!" I call into the mic hooked around my ears. "You'll only get out what you put in, so werk it! Crank it up!"

A rush runs through me when everyone reaches for the red resistance knobs on their bikes. There are at least a dozen glowers in the class, some guys grunt as the machines force them to use every last ounce of their energy. And still, these guys come back day after day, week after week to let me torture them.

Sometimes, I love my job.

"I want two full turns of your resistance. Don't give up

on me now, bitches. Because we're climbing in four, three, two, one. And climb!"

Everyone rises out of their seats, swaying side-to-side as they use their full body weight to turn the pedals. They all look like they're in pain. Everyone is soaked with sweat. This is going to be my best class of the week.

Thirty minutes later, after I've led the class through a cool down and reminded them to hydrate, I unclip myself from my bike and hop off.

"Donnie, bro, that was a killer class." A big burly guy comes up for a manly shoulder hug and a slap on the back.

I try to hide my grimace as my wet shoulder makes contact with his. "Thanks, bro."

"You used a new song in there, right?" Another guy asks, face flushed so red I wonder if I should be concerned.

"The interval set? Yeah, that's a new one. Good catch."

"Hey, Donnie, I'm looking to buy new cycling shoes. Have any you'd recommend?"

I get caught up in a discussion about shoes with the stiffest soles, and by the time the guy is satisfied, the room has cleared out. I grab my phone, shut down the sound system, and go to the staff locker room for a shower.

Beau and Gavin are there when I round the row of lockers. They're standing flush against each other, Gavin's arms around Beau's neck and Beau's arms around Gavin's hips. Their heads are bent in close as they whisper into the tiny space they've created between them.

It's not unusual to find them intimate like this around the gym. Still, my heart aches a little bit every time I see them.

"Get a room, girls," I joke.

They pull apart, though Beau's hand lingers at the small of Gavin's back.

"Hey, is what's his name still staying with you?" Beau asks.

My pulse spikes at the mention of Connor and I take a moment to open my locker and toss my shoes inside. "Connor? Yeah, he is. Why?"

"Just checking to see how things are going," Beau says.

He sounds nonchalant, but I know he's checking up on me. He and Gavin were incredibly supportive when Roger passed. They let me take a leave of absence from the gym, stopped in to make sure I ate and showered, and when the time was right, they dragged me back to work. I wouldn't have made it through those first few months without them.

Which makes the way I treated Beau the other day inexcusable. But also... sex with Connor yesterday had been... really fucking good. It wasn't just the mind-blowing orgasms, it was how fun it was, how comfortable we were in the afterglow. We went downstairs and Connor sorted through some of his bags while I made dinner. Then we ate, washed up, and watched a movie all curled up on the couch. It was sweet, cozy, relaxing. It felt like something we've done a dozen times, rather than only a handful.

At bedtime, we stood outside Connor's room and kissed each other goodnight. A gentle, tender kiss that left me smiling all the way to bed. I fell asleep with that smile on my lips. I woke up with it too.

It was only when I went into the walk-in closet this morning to get dressed that I had a sudden bout of doubt. Seeing Roger's clothes, feeling the weight of my wedding ring, guilt trickled in. I shouldn't sleep with Connor while I'm still wearing my ring, right? That's the least I can do. And yet, I can't take it off. Not quite yet.

"Things are good," I say, trying to sound as nonchalant as Beau does. "He's probably going to stay with me for a while." I brought it up over dinner last night and Connor agreed, on the condition that he gets to pay me rent. I don't need the rental income, but I understand why it's important to him.

Beau and Gavin exchange a look and they aren't at all subtle about it.

"Really?" Gavin slides onto the bench next to me. "How long is a while?"

"I dunno." I shrug. A smile tugs at the corner of my lips. "A while."

Gavin shoots a glance at Beau, then looks back at me. "You fucked him, didn't you?"

My cheeks heat and there's nothing I can do to stop it.

"Shut up!" Gavin shoves me hard enough that I almost topple over. "You did!"

"Maybe."

"Are you sure that's a good idea?" Beau's got his arms crossed over his chest, making him look huge. He leans against the locker next to mine and the two of them effectively box me in.

"Why wouldn't it be a good idea?" Gavin asks for me. "Do you know how long he's been celibate?"

I roll my eyes. "It hasn't been that long." Except it has. I haven't felt the need to get it on with anyone until Connor.

"The guy just broke up with his ex, didn't he? And the ex came looking for him?" Beau cocks an eyebrow at me and I can see why he's concerned.

"It's over between them," I assure him.

"Still, it's a little fast."

I tamp down the annoyance rising inside me. It's the same thing Miles said and I hate that Beau somehow keeps bringing out the same reactions in me as that slimy bastard.

"I don't want you to get hurt."

"You think he's using our Donnie as a rebound?" Gavin asks.

I flinch. It's the same worry I had when I first started feeling this attraction to Connor. If I'm honest, I'm still a little worried about it. In the grand scheme of things, I don't actually know Connor at all—I met him barely a week ago. I've been going off my gut feelings with him, acting more out of instinct than reason.

Gavin and Beau are both watching me, waiting for a response I don't have.

"Guys, it's fine. Really." I start stripping out of my cycling gear. "We enjoy each other's company, that's all. I'm not going to…" To what? Marry him? My stomach flips over on itself. "We're just having fun. There's nothing to worry about."

I wrap a clean towel around my waist and give Beau a pointed look. He stares me down for a moment before moving out of my way.

"I appreciate your concern though," I say, on my way to the showers. "Thank you."

"Just be careful!" Gavin calls after me and I wave back at them in acknowledgment.

I don't feel the need to be careful. Maybe it's naïve of me, maybe it's foolhardy, maybe I'm too infatuated to think straight, but I really don't think Connor will hurt me.

I shower quickly and Beau and Gavin are nowhere in sight when I finish. I change and wave to Sawyer on my way out. He gives me a sly smile and an eyebrow wiggle. Word travels ridiculously fast around here. I roll my eyes and rush home.

Connor's sitting at the dining table in the kitchen when I walk in. He's wearing headphones and scowling at his computer. I sit down next to him and his face brightens like he's been waiting for me to come home.

"Hey, how was your day?" he asks, pulling his headphones down around his neck.

"Good, all my classes were full."

Connor looks amused. "Your classes are always full, Donnie, The Spin Instructor."

I groan and shake my head. "Not you too."

Connor giggles and the sound wraps around me like a warm, fuzzy blanket.

"How was *your* day?"

Connor sobers. "I emailed one of my old instructors from film school. You know, about the grant." He slumps down into his chair and runs his finger along the edge of the table.

"And?"

"And he wasn't very helpful."

"What did he say?" I prod.

"That the grant is a great opportunity, but if it doesn't work out for whatever reason, there will be other grants in the future." His bottom lip is nice and plump as he sticks it out, and all I want to do is take it between my lips and tug.

"Have you had a chance to talk to your boss?"

Connor shakes his head. "I have a feeling he's going to tell me the same thing."

It all comes back to whether he's willing to work with Wyatt, and after our excursion to his old apartment, I'm firmly in the no camp. "I can see where your instructor is coming from."

Connor glances at me skeptically and waits for me to continue.

"There will be other opportunities in the future. There always are. It's not like there's a deadline on these types of things."

Connor's pout turns into a scowl. "There kinda is."

I think I know where this is going and I don't like it. "What deadline?" I ask, a little more forcefully than I need to.

He hesitates, studying me, like he knows how I'm going to react. I keep my face as neutral as possible, but I don't do a very good job.

"Well, when I turn thirty," he mumbles.

Yep, there it is. "That's not a deadline, darling."

Connor's scowl deepens, but he doesn't argue with me. He knows I'm right. He just doesn't believe it. I understand, I've been there before.

"Do you know what I did before I started teaching spin?"

Connor perks up. "No."

"I worked in banking."

His eyebrows shoot to his hairline. "Really?"

"Really. I hated it. It was boring. The hours were ridiculously long. I had no life outside the office. Spin was just starting to pop up in some gyms and it was the only way I could get a break from work." That and Roger. The familiar aching pain expands in my chest and I force myself to breathe through it.

"So you quit your high-powered bank job and became a spin instructor."

"That's right."

"How old were you then?"

I count out the years in my head. "Twenty-seven? Twenty-eight?"

"I'm twenty-six."

I tilt my head to the side. "See? You still have plenty of time."

His pout is back. "Still feels like I'm running out of it."

He sounds so dejected, like things are so utterly dire. It's such a mid-twenties reaction that I'm simultaneously smitten and annoyed. Oh, to be that young again when everything feels so big and consequential. Where every decision seems so final and the fear of getting it wrong is very real.

Connor really is a lot younger than I am and in that moment, I feel quite old. Worn and weathered with decades of life experiences under my belt that he doesn't share, that he might not understand.

Does that matter? Beau and Gavin seem to think it might. Me? I'm not so sure.

"If you and Wyatt stop working together, would you still be eligible for the grant on your own?"

Connor's brow furrows as he thinks. "I don't know. Even if I am, I don't think Wyatt would let me just take over the whole thing."

I nod. That makes sense. "Okay, so if you don't go ahead with the grant, do you have other projects or scripts you're working on?"

He scrunches up his face. "Sorta. There's a bunch of

half-baked ideas on my hard drive, but none of them are any good."

"But they're there. And you'll think of new ideas."

"I guess."

"You can still write scripts and make movies after you turn thirty."

"I know."

"It's not like we shrivel up and turn into stone after thirty." I point to myself because, hey, I'm not called Donnie, The Spin Instructor, for no reason.

Connor throws me a glare with a grin tugging at his lips. "I know. It's just that there's a lot of competition out there. There're so many thirty under thirty genius directors already and I'm... I've got nothing."

I hold out my hand and he puts his in it. "Life's not a competition, darling. It's not a race. We stop and start all the time. We can change directions at any point." What I'm saying is so common sense and yet it feels like I'm hearing them for the first time.

I can stop and start again. I can change directions at any point. I'm not done with living just because I'm a certain age and lost my life partner. I'm not relegated to merely existing. The words echo through me and the truth of them hurts me to the core. My thumb goes to my wedding ring.

I am moving forward though, aren't I? Slower than a glacier perhaps, but it is happening. Because of Connor.

He's here for a reason. Maybe so I can help him through a tough time. Maybe so he can lure me back into life again. Even if it's only for a season and then we go our separate ways, I know, deep down, that this is what we both need right now.

CONNOR

I get off the subway in Midtown and walk toward the hotel where I'm supposed to meet my boss, Rick. My eyes are glued to the sidewalk under my feet and my hood is pulled up over my head to keep out this last blast of winter.

After dinner last night, we had another session of *Remedy Donnie's Woeful Knowledge of Popular Films* and watched *Casablanca*. No more giant bowls of popcorn to cock block us. We curled up nice and close on the couch, me big-spooning Donnie, tucked in under a blanket.

Donnie fell asleep halfway through—slacker.

There was a moment on the second-floor landing when we were on our way to bed. I was in front of my room and Donnie had one foot on the step leading up to his on the third floor. I held my breath, heart racing, waiting for Donnie to decide what to do.

We hadn't done anything more than some kissing and cuddling all evening, but that was enough for my dick to get presumptuous. It'd been more than a little chubby during the movie and there was no way Donnie hadn't felt it on the couch.

Still, I wanted him to initiate. Things aren't at all cut and dry between us. I'm not so naïve to believe that just because I broke up with Miles, I don't still have shit I need to work through. And then, there's Roger.

I feel a lot more comfortable in the house now. It's starting to feel like home. Every now and then though, I'm reminded of Roger and how his presence still lingers here. In the wedding ring Donnie hasn't taken off. In the office across from my room. I don't know how Donnie feels about all that. I'm a little afraid to ask.

Donnie gave me a goodnight kiss before he went upstairs. It was sweet, with just enough heat that I melted in his arms. When he pulled away, there was a promise in his eyes that settled my heart and let me breathe. I lay in bed afterward with the lights off and the door closed, wondering what Donnie was doing upstairs. I woke up this morning wishing I had him in my arms. He met me downstairs with a bowl of overnight oats and a thorough good morning kiss.

We have time. There's no rush. Neither of us is going anywhere.

A hand grabs my arm and I spin around, hand raised to fend off my attacker.

"Hey, it's just me."

I sigh, heart pounding, all senses on high alert. "Jesus, Rick, you scared the crap out of me."

He shrugs like reaching out and grabbing random strangers is something he does every day. "I called your name. You walked right past me."

I look up and see the hotel's entrance is half a block behind us. "Oh, sorry. I was distracted."

"Yeah, no shit. Come on." Rick leads me back to the hotel and the dimly lit lobby.

The place is sleek and trendy with shiny white tiles on the floor and shiny white panels on the walls. Oddly shaped lights hang from the ceiling, glowing pink, then blue, then purple. White stuffed couches sit next to several of those giant egg-shaped chairs.

A hotel manager meets us by the reception desk. We were hired to produce new videos and photographs for their website, and now we're here to scope out the place and design a production plan. Jackson, the manager, takes us up to one of the guest rooms. The suite we're in is large and has the same vibes as the lobby. All white. Space age-y. Kinda bland except for the view.

It faces west out over the Hudson River toward New Jersey. The late winter sun reflects off the water, making it shimmer. The sunset from here would be amazing. If I put a couple actors by the window, I'll get some fantastic silhouettes.

My phone buzzes and I pull it out of my pocket. Maybe it's Donnie, checking in. Maybe he wants to see if I want spaghetti squash or zucchini noodles for dinner.

It's Wyatt. He must be fed up with waiting for me. Well, he can wait a little longer. I send it to voicemail.

Two seconds later, a text message comes through.

WYATT

You can't ignore me forever.

I know I can't, but I haven't figured out what I want to do yet.

WYATT

> If I don't hear from you, I'm going to
> respond to the granting committee and
> take the interview myself.

Wait a fucking minute. He can't do that. It's *my* script. I wrote most of it. I'm the creative brains behind the whole thing. I smash my finger on the call button. Wyatt picks up on the second ring.

"Thought that would get your attention," he says by way of greeting.

"Are you fucking kidding me?" I escape to a corner of the suite so Rick and Jackson won't hear me.

"Connor." Wyatt sounds like he's speaking to a toddler throwing a temper tantrum.

"That script is mine. There's no fucking way I'm letting you steal it from me."

"What? I'm not stealing anything. The script is *ours*. We're *partners*. I want us to do the interview together."

I laugh, hard and bitter. I was on the fence about whether I could keep working with Wyatt, but hearing him act like nothing happened, I know there is absolutely no way.

"I'm not doing the interview with you and I'm not letting you do it alone. First, you steal my boyfriend, now you're trying to steal my script. Who knows what else you'll steal next."

"Jesus Christ, Connor, I'm not stealing anything."

"Then why were you fucking my boyfriend behind my back?" I'm doing a bad job of not shouting. The suite is silent behind me. I stuff myself deeper into the corner.

"It's not what you think."

I scoff, disgusted. "That's a tired line."

"It's true." Wyatt sighs heavily into the phone. "We love each other."

I stare at the white wall in front of me, feeling like I've taken an icy cold knife deep into the softest part of my gut. I can't move. I can't breathe. I'm paralyzed, my brain caught in a do-not-compute over what Wyatt's saying.

What does he mean they love each other? How? Since when?

It comes to me piece by piece. Me coming home to find them hanging out together, watching movies on the couch, laughing in the kitchen, reading quietly next to each other. They were always so understanding when I needed to work odd hours or got called in unexpectedly. They never complained.

Wyatt turning away when I went to kiss Miles. Miles keeping his hands to himself when Wyatt was around. I thought Wyatt was just giving us some privacy. I thought Miles didn't want to make him uncomfortable.

All that time, they were in love with each other and trying to hide it from me. I'm the dupe, the delusional one. I was living in my own little make-believe world. It's so obvious now that I can't believe I didn't see it before.

"Connor?"

I start like Wyatt smacked me in the face.

"Connor, say something."

There's nothing to say. They have each other now, they don't need anything else from me.

"No, it's over. Tell the granting committee we're pulling our application." I hang up and collapse with my shoulder against the wall, trying to keep down the breakfast Donnie made for me.

"What's going on?" Rick comes up behind me.

I straighten, swallowing down bile. "Nothing, sorry. I'm fine."

"Clearly, you're not fine. What the hell was that?" Rick gestures to my phone.

"Wyatt."

Rick stares at me blankly.

"My best friend." I cringe at the words. "Ex-friend. Ex-creative partner."

Rick seems to pick up on the "ex" part and some of the annoyance drops from his tone. "Is this going to be a problem?"

I shake my head. "No."

"Good."

I follow Rick and Jackson through the rest of the tour, taking reference photos with my phone and jotting down notes about lighting and camera angles. It's a good distraction that keeps my mind off the call with Wyatt. But by the time we're done, Wyatt and the grant is the only thing I can think about again.

Why did I tell him to pull the application? I've just tanked my career before it's even started. I'm never going to get another grant after this.

"Hey, Rick," I say when Jackson leaves us in the hotel lobby. Anxiety skitters across my skin and I'm all jittery and antsy.

"Yeah?"

"Can I, um, talk to you about something?"

We go to a Starbucks down the street and grab the last empty table in the corner. I can barely sit still.

"So, um, how bad is it if I've applied for a production grant and then pull my application halfway through the process?"

Rick cocks an eyebrow. "Huh? What do you mean?"

Fuck. I don't want to go into the whole backstory with Miles and Wyatt. I just want to know how much of a self-sabotaging idiot I am.

"Does this have anything to do with the call earlier?" Rick asks.

"Yeah, it does."

"Okay, so spill."

I don't know how else to spill without telling him everything. It's humiliating, but I do, starting from the script Wyatt and I were working on, straight through the cheating and the email from the granting committee, ending with the call he overheard.

Rick's silent the entire time, his expression inscrutable.

"So… I guess I'm wondering… how fucked am I?"

Rick takes a long sip of his flat white. "I dunno what to tell ya. Life's hard. This industry is harder. Shit is going to hit the fan every other day. There are assholes around every fucking corner and you don't always have the luxury of choosing who you work with."

I frown, my stomach twisting into knots so tight I think I'm going to be sick. "So I'm really fucked."

"Is anyone ever really fucked?" Rick shrugs. "I mean, yeah, this grant sounds like it's a big deal. But guess what? There are hundreds of grants out there."

That's kinda exactly what my film school instructor said. Kinda what Donnie said too.

"Listen, kid. There's never a clear-cut answer to any of this. Is this the big break you've been waiting for? Maybe, who can say? Is it worth it if you've gotta work with someone you don't like? Only you can answer that. The only way you're ever truly fucked, is if you stop trying."

Rick checks the time on his phone. "Hey, I gotta jet. I'll see ya tomorrow, 'kay?"

I stay behind to finish my latte with a double pump of hazelnut syrup. I know everything Rick said is right. Donnie too. In my head, it makes perfect sense. If anyone else came to me, I'd tell them the same thing.

So why doesn't it *feel* right? Why does it feel like everything is slipping through my fingers and the harder I try to hold on, the less I have to grasp?

DONNIE

I find Connor downstairs in the theater room when I get home in the evening. He's curled up in a ball, staring at the screen.

"Hey, what are you watching?"

He holds out his hand and when I take it, he drags me onto the couch with him. He settles his head in my lap and my fingers immediately go to his hair. I think this is going to be my new favorite thing, playing with his hair. He hums whenever I comb my fingers through it. He gasps whenever I rake my nails across his scalp.

"I don't know."

"You don't know what you're watching?"

He shrugs. His eyes are closed. I go on high alert. Something's wrong.

"Did something happen today?"

Connor turns onto his side and buries his face into my stomach, his arm curls around my waist, holding us together. My heart rate spikes instantly and that rage monster I've developed cracks his knuckles.

Connor mumbles something against my stomach.

"What was that, darling?" I try to lean back so I can hear what he's saying, but Connor tugs me closer.

"Wyatt called me," he says, a little louder. "Or I called Wyatt or whatever."

Christ, of course it has to do with Wyatt or Miles. They just can't leave Connor alone, can they? "What did he want?

"He said they're in love."

I don't know how to feel about that. Shitty because of what it means for Connor. Good riddance since Connor doesn't need them anymore. He's got me. Either way, it's no excuse for sleeping together behind his back. "Is that supposed to make what they did okay?"

Connor shoots up and spins to face me. "That's what I said! He actually wants to do the grant interview together! Can you believe it? Together!"

My anger is chomping at the bit and I curl my fingers into the couch cushion in a feeble attempt to keep myself grounded. "What did you tell him?" My voice sounds surprisingly level, considering the amount of adrenaline coursing through my system.

"I told him to go fuck himself!"

My lips twitch. It's not funny, but it's pretty funny. "Yeah, you did."

"Yeah! I did!" Connor's eyes are bright and his cheeks are flushed with color. He's breathing hard and vibrating with energy like he's in the middle of one of my classes. He's gorgeous and I want to drag him straight to bed.

Then suddenly, he deflates like someone yanked the plug on him. "I told Wyatt to pull our grant application."

Shit. "Oh, darling, I'm so sorry."

He shrugs, though it looks more like a full-body slump. "Yeah, well."

I pull him to me, head on my shoulder, and I press a kiss to the top of his head.

"I talked to Rick about it. He says there will be other grants."

Whoever this Rick is, I approve. "He's right. There will be."

"It's just…"

"I know," I say when Connor trails off. "It's hard, I know."

Connor lifts his head to look up at me. His eyes aren't as bright as they were a moment before, but there's something else in them now. A heat that ripples through me and settles in my groin.

I kiss him. I trace the curve of that plump bottom lip of his with my tongue, then draw it into my mouth to suck on it. He gasps and lets out a low needy sound. My hands are in his hair, holding him at the right angle as I swipe my tongue over his. He swipes back and we're licking at each other until my head spins.

"Donnie," he says with such vulnerability that my entire body reacts.

My dick is hard, my pulse is racing, my skin breaks out in goosebumps. He needs me and I want him and in this moment, nothing else matters.

I grab the back of his shirt and tug. Connor bends and the shirt comes right off him. I toss it away. He unzips my light jacket, pushes it off my shoulders, then takes the hem of my Mars t-shirt and pulls it over my head.

The light from the screen flickers over Connor's body. He's not ripped like so many of the other men at Mars. He's wide and solid and he's got a precious layer of padding around his middle. I run my fingers over him, loving how his body moves and bunches under my touch. He has this light blond fuzz everywhere—his shoulders, his forearms, his back—that makes me want to pet and stroke him all night.

I push him onto his back and straddle him. I pinch his nipples and he jolts like I've electrocuted him. His dick is hard in his jeans and I roll my hips, feeling it grow under me. I lift one of his arms and lick into the sensitive curves there.

"Donnie!" He wriggles and tries to pull him arm down while trying to push my head in deeper at the same time.

I do it again. There's something so intimate about a man's armpits. So many nerve-endings and yet so often ignored. A man's scent there is potent and raw, unfiltered and primal. I could spend hours painting Connor's pits with my tongue.

"Donnie, please!"

Especially when he begs me so prettily like that.

I switch to his other arm, finding every little dip, nipping at every fold of skin. Connor's sobbing. He can't hold still. He's almost bucking us right off the couch. I kiss him, pushing my tongue into his mouth, letting him taste himself on me. He moans and sucks on my tongue and I maybe come a little in my sweats.

"Please, Donnie, let me fuck you. Please."

Well, when he asks so politely. I jump off him and pull

him to his feet. We sprint up the stairs and I skid to a stop on the second floor. My stomach drops. "I don't have condoms." And if I did, they'd for sure be expired.

"I do." Connor pushes past me into his room and starts rummaging through his gym bags. Thank god for twenty-somethings who never leave the house without supplies.

I drop my sweats and underwear and climb onto the bed. When Connor turns to me, the look that comes over his face makes my breath hitch in my chest. He's studying me like I'm a masterpiece and he's a devoted art history student. He steps out of his jeans and climbs up from the foot of the bed.

His gaze is hot as it trails up my legs and lingers on my cock. It's hard and leaking. My balls are already drawn up tight. He ghosts his fingers over my hips, down one side and up the other, then he does it again and my hips come off the bed.

Connor's eyes flick to mine. His got that lip of his caught between his teeth, and when he looks at me through his lashes like that, fuck, it's too much. I reach for him and he covers me with his body. So big, so heavy. I spread my legs and his hips settle right down between them. I take that lip from him. If he gets to chew on it, then I want to chew on it too.

Connor moans and jerks. His hot, thick cock brushes along mine. Goddamn, I want that thing inside me. I want it stretching me open and filling me up. I want to feel his hip bones hitting my ass, driving me into the mattress. I want to be sore afterward. I want to walk funny tomorrow.

"Connor, fuck me."

He sits back and fumbles for the condom. I take the moment to flip onto my stomach, drawing my knees under me so my ass is in the air. Christ, it's been a long time since I've put myself in this kind of position, since I've opened myself up to someone else like this. My cheeks are hot at how wanton I feel. My dick throbs at the lewd image I must present.

Connor's hands run up the backs of my thighs. They cover my ass, give them a squeeze, then pull them apart. The air is cold on my hole.

"Holy shit." Connor's breath is hot on it.

I quiver, needing him, his tongue, his cock, his body. "Connor."

He licks a quick swipe across my hole. I let out a high-pitch whine. He does it again, and I whine even higher. Connor twirls his tongue around and around the entrance to my body until I'm blabbering into the sheets and arching up for more. Then his tongue is pushing into me and I sob with relief.

It's wet and weird and I've forgotten how fucking good it feels. Connor takes his time opening me up and my heart swells with tenderness for him. I'm tight and unpracticed after so many years and it takes me a few minutes to remember how to let someone inside. When he pushes a lubed finger into me, my body screams with pleasure, and I almost come with that tiny penetration. When he pushes in another, the pain of the stretch only adds to the sparks firing all over me.

He fucks me with his fingers and his tongue, finding my prostate and massaging it from the inside. It's too good, too much, and I swear I'm going to fucking come like that. He needs to get his cock in me now or he's not going to at all tonight.

"Please, Connor. Hurry."

He pulls away and a moment later, I feel the blunt tip of his dick against my hole. There's pressure against me, but I'm too tight. The pressure increases and for a second I'm mortified that this isn't going to work. I breathe deep, remind myself to relax, and when he presses in again, I bear down. The head of his cock slips into me and holy fucking shit, I feel like I'm flying apart.

Connor leans over me, covering me with his big body, pinning me down with his weight. I muffle my sobs with a pillow. It's not only how incredibly good it feels to have him in me, it's more than the physical sensation. He's brought my body back to life. He's showing me that there's more to living than merely going through the same daily routine. He's reminding me that it's never too late to start over, to try something new, to take risks.

He rocks slowly, gently, inching deeper and deeper into me. When he's fully seated, we're both trembling, teetering on the edge. I'm full. It's staggering. My dick is pulsing and I feel it from the roots of my hair to the soles of my feet. I'm not going to last long. I don't even want to try.

"Fuck me, Connor. Hard. Fast. Make me come."

Connor growls in my ear. He pulls halfway out and slams back in. *That's it. Exactly like that. Tear me apart. Ruin me.*

Connor fucks me. I'm flat on my stomach. His arm is wrapped over my shoulder and across my chest. I dig my fingers into his forearms and hang on for dear life. His cock is pistoning in and out of my ass, hard and fast, just like I asked for. Sweat drips off him and onto me. Every lungful of air I suck in smells like fucking sex. And in the midst of our bodies crashing together over and over again, a peace settles over me.

This is right. This is good. This is as it should be.

Something special has developed between us, something we need to cherish and nurture. It's going to end well. I know it in the deepest parts of me.

My orgasm is almost an afterthought, just pleasure surging through nerves that are already overloaded. I don't scream. I don't sob. I think I'm smiling into the pillow as I ride the wave.

Above me, Connor comes too. He sinks deep into me and his whole-body contracts around me. It's wonderful. I love it. I want to stay like this forever.

CONNOR

It's late by the time our legs are strong enough to hold us. I try to convince Donnie to order takeout, but he's insistent about cooking. It's quinoa this time, with some chicken that's been marinating in the fridge.

I'm sitting at the island, pretending to work on my laptop when I'm really watching Donnie move around the kitchen. He looks like he's dancing, floating from the sink to the cutting board to the stove and back. He holds a knife like it's an extension of his arm. Every movement is fluid and graceful.

I want to set up cameras and try to capture the way he cooks on film. The way he glides. The sharp chops of the knife against the cutting board, the confident scrape as he scoops up the veggies and dumps them into a bowl. The excited sizzle when he drops the chicken into the hot oil. The curl of steam rising from the pan.

I'm not sure I could do it justice. I desperately want to try.

Donnie tends to play with his wedding ring. It isn't the first time I've noticed him twirling it around and around. He probably doesn't even realize he's doing it. It makes me think of Roger. Did he ever sit here watching Donnie cook? I can't imagine anyone not wanting to.

What else did he and Donnie do together? What was he like? This man who Donnie shared a life with, who Donnie loved. I want to know. I want to... I don't know, see how I measure up or something.

"What was Roger like?" I ask, before I lose my nerve. We're both kinda buzzed from the sex earlier and if I don't ask now, I might not have the courage to do it later. "If you don't mind me asking about him."

Donnie looks surprised, but not upset. He flattens his left hand on the counter and the ring gives off a dull *clink* when it makes contact with the hard surface.

"I don't mind," he says, then stares into the distance for a moment. "Roger was a force of nature. Once he decided to do something, nothing could stop him and he wouldn't quit until he got what he wanted. It... got pretty annoying sometimes."

Donnie laughs, his eyes crinkling at the edges, like he's remembering a particularly annoying incident. He pulls out plates and scoops steaming mounds of quinoa onto each.

"He was funny. Always the life of the party. Also, a workaholic. Always staying late at the office and then bringing work home. We turned one of the bedrooms into a home office for him..." He trails off.

Ah, shit. I need to tell him. "Actually," I say, heat rising up my neck and onto my cheeks. "I kinda stumbled onto it."

Donnie turns to me like he might not have heard what I said. "Roger's office?"

I nod.

He ducks his head and turns away. My heart aches for him.

"I'm so sorry. I wasn't trying to snoop or anything. I wasn't thinking and opened the door and… I didn't touch anything, I swear." God, I feel fucking awful.

Donnie smiles sadly while carrying the plates over to the table. "It's okay. I'm the one who should be embarrassed."

"Why?" I bring over the cutlery and Donnie grabs our drinks.

"It's been almost four years," he says, not meeting my eyes. "And… I have a closet full of his clothes, too."

The ache in my chest grows deeper.

"I should have sorted through all his things ages ago. It's just…" He pokes at the chicken on his plate. "This sounds stupid. His things were all I had left of him and… it felt like the only way I could keep a piece of him with me."

"That's not stupid."

"I know they're just things." Donnie's voice is thick with emotion now and I hate that I've ruined our evening. "I know I'll still remember him without them. But the longer I put it off, the harder it was to do it."

"I'm sorry. We don't have to talk about this." Let's rewind the last five minutes and I'll start over again with something less fraught.

"It's okay." Donnie sniffles and finally looks at me. His eyes are glassy, but his smile is more nostalgic than sad. "I should have forced myself to clean his things out ages ago. I just need to… force myself to do it."

"I…" Am probably overstepping my bounds, but I don't like how lonely Donnie sounds right now. "… can help. If you want."

He blinks at me. "Really? You'd do that?"

I shrug. I can't think of a reason why I wouldn't. "Yeah, sure. I mean, you helped me with all my shit. I can help you with…" I almost call Roger's things shit. *Shit.* "Uh, I mean…"

Donnie chuckles and the air suddenly feels lighter between us. "I know what you mean. And thank you. I appreciate it."

On the island behind us, my phone buzzes. I ignore it and it buzzes again.

"Do you need to get that?"

"Naw, it's fine." There's literally no one in my life who can't wait until I finish dinner with Donnie.

My phone buzzes again and again and again.

"Are you sure?"

I groan and throw my head back. There's only one person in the world who would text me twenty messages in a row like that. I grab my phone off the counter and bring it back to the table.

BRAD

Mom and dad's anniversary is in a few weeks.

Don't forget.

Put it in your calendar.

You need to be here by Friday.

We're having family dinner on Friday.

The big party is on Saturday.

You're not allowed to leave until Sunday.

I roll my eyes and set it face down on the table.

"Who is it?" Donnie looks concerned.

"No one. Just my brother."

"Oh, I didn't know you have a brother."

"I do. An annoying one."

Donnie's lips twitch. "What does he want?"

"To make sure I go home for my parent's anniversary in a few weeks," I grumble. I scoop some quinoa and a piece of chicken and stuff it in my mouth. The chicken is really, really good. The quinoa is... good with the chicken.

"You don't want to go?" Donnie's making good headway on his plate of food and I hurry to catch up.

"It's not that I don't want to. It's just... a hassle."

Donnie's lips twitch into a grin. "A hassle?

It's hard for me to explain because it's not any single thing that bothers me about visiting them. My parents are good parents. My brother is... ugh, my brother. I had a great childhood—absolutely no complaints. Even now, I know I can always go to my parents if I need help with anything. My brother is, you know, my brother, but he'll always drop what he's doing if I call him.

Except every time we're in the same room, we tend to

end up in epic arguments over I don't even know what. Silly things, stupid things—I don't do laundry often enough, why don't I move to a cheaper neighborhood, I shouldn't eat so much takeout.

Donnie would get along great with my mom on that last point.

It's stuff that no one is right about, so no one can win, and then we just go around and around until someone—usually me—storms out. It's exhausting. It also sounds petty.

"Well, I have to take the train up there and I don't have a car, so I'm stuck at my parents' house all weekend."

Donnie's looking at me like I have to be joking. It's a weak excuse and I know it.

"Where do they live?"

"Springfield, Massachusetts, not Illinois."

Donnie furrows his brow. "Is that a small town?"

I'm not surprised that he doesn't know it. New Yorkers, am I right? "No, it's a city, but it's mostly suburbs."

He nods. "So it's mainly a transportation issue." He's too smart for my own good.

"No, it's more than that."

He takes a bite and looks at me while he chews, waiting for me to continue.

I huff dramatically, throwing all my acting chops into it. "We argue about nothing and I don't even know why."

"You don't get along?"

I scrunch up my face. "We don't not get along."

"You're adorable, darling, but you're not making any sense."

I flush. I know I'm not making any sense, but Donnie

called me adorable and now I want to giggle. "What about you? Do you get along with your family?"

Donnie's smile freezes on his face and oh god, I've done it again, haven't I? He drops his gaze to his plate.

"We don't have to talk about it. Sorry, I'm sorry."

He shakes his head and tries to grin. It looks painful more than anything else. "My family's all back in London. We're not close. In fact, I haven't spoken to them in years."

I want to know why. I don't dare ask. I stuff more quinoa and chicken in my mouth.

Donnie wipes his lips with his napkin and sets it aside. "They didn't take my coming out very well. This was in the nineties, in the middle of the AIDS epidemic. They basically told me that if I insisted on being gay, then I could find myself somewhere else to live." He pauses for a moment, then clears his throat.

"So I came to America, met Roger, and…" He holds his hand out, palms up, then drops them back into his lap.

"Fuck, I'm sorry." I feel awful, like a spoiled, ungrateful brat who doesn't appreciate what he has.

Donnie's gone through so much, survived so much. Losing the love of his life. Having his own family kick him out. I don't have a fraction of a clue what any of that is like. I can't even imagine it. I don't have anything I can say, nothing to share that can make him feel better.

And Roger. He sounds like a really cool guy. Smart and funny and successful. I would never measure up to that. I'm a kid compared to him—compared to Donnie. So what exactly do I think I'm doing here? Trying to fill Roger's shoes? Good god, I am delusional. There's no way in hell I'll be able to do that.

"It's life," Donnie says, softly, gazing at some spot on

the other side of the room. "There are highs and lows. You don't get the happy moments without the sad ones."

"But you've had so many sad ones."

Donnie's eyes dart to mine and he grins indulgently. "I've had a lot more time to accumulate them than you have. I have a lot more happy ones too."

That's the whole point, isn't it? Donnie's older, mature, sophisticated. I'm young and inexperienced and naïve. What could I possibly have to offer him? What could he possibly see in me?

CONNOR

We kind of fall into a routine, but instead of being mundane, it almost feels like I'm on the verge of something big. I've never felt more energized in my life—though, maybe that has something to do with all the healthy eating Donnie's foisted on me and all the extra spin classes I've been going to. Donnie's taken to saving a bike for me, which means I *have* to show up, and I'm not mad about it.

It's a little weird, to be honest, how peppy and focused and *on* I am. I fly through work stuff so fast that Rick jokingly asked if I was taking Adderall or something. I'm not. I'm just high on, I don't know, Donnie maybe. Between breakfast and dinner, spin classes and movie nights, we manage to go see the cherry blossoms in the park, stroll through art fairs, and ogle hot sailors during Fleet Week. At night, Donnie takes me apart with his tongue and when I sink into him, it feels like I'm coming home.

I'm writing too. So much, so fast. The scenes are coming to me fully formed, like I'm already seeing them on the screen. It's a completely new story about a gay couple who inherit an old dilapidated house from a myste-rious great aunt, only to find that the house is haunted—guess how I came up with that idea.

For the first time in my life, I feel in control. I know what I'm doing. I know where I'm going. It's just a matter of doing the work and getting there.

"So, um, I was thinking," I say one evening as we're cleaning up after dinner. "I should go get tested."

It's been niggling at the back of my mind for a while now. Miles and I didn't use condoms and god knows what he and Wyatt were doing.

Donnie's standing at the sink, staring at the backsplash with the faucet on and a wet tea towel in his hand. He's been kinda distracted all through dinner, not saying much, his smiles not quite reaching his eyes. He looks tired. He says he's had a long day, but I've never seen him this out of it before.

"Donnie?" I put my hand on his shoulder and he jumps.

"Huh? Sorry, what was that?"

"Are you okay?" Worry trickles into me. We've been on such a high and honeymoon periods don't last forever.

"Yeah." He shakes his head, turns off the water, and wrings out the tea towel. "I'm okay. What did you say?"

I don't believe him. There's something up and I know it. We've talked about a lot of serious stuff during the time we've known each other, and I'm not used to this feeling of him shutting me out.

"I said I was thinking about getting tested. You know, with Miles and Wyatt and all that…"

He nods and steps away from me to wipe down the counter next to the sink. It already looks clean to me. "Sure, great idea."

My worry grows into something sharper and spikier. My mind starts jumping to all sorts of conclusions—is he sick? Did something happen at Mars?

I try to close the distance between us. "Do you want to come with me?"

"Uh, I…" He goes around the island to the kitchen table and wipes it down. Again.

"Donnie?" The spikes have morphed into fear now. Something's seriously wrong. Does he regret getting involved with me? Does he want me to move out? "Please, Donnie. You're scaring me."

His eyes dart to mine and he blinks a few times before he focuses on my face. He sighs, and the tension drains from his body. "I'm so sorry, it's…" He swallows like he's trying to clear his throat.

"You can tell me. Please," I beg.

He lifts a hand and places it on my cheek. It's wet and cold but I hold it to my face anyway. His eyes are soft and tender and so sweet that my heart expands in my chest. I love it when he looks at me like that, like I'm precious and he can't believe I'm here.

He takes my hand and leads me to the living room where we settle on the couch. He flips the fireplace on, even though it's probably too warm for it. I'm tucked into a corner and Donnie fits right between my legs, his back against my chest. We melt into each other.

This is my favorite way of holding him. This and

straight up spooning him from behind. He feels so good fitted against me like we were made for each other.

"It's the anniversary of Roger's death," he whispers.

I close my eyes and press a kiss to the spot where his jaw meets his ear. All the fear from a moment ago dissolves into hurt for Donnie. It's not about me—*not everything is, genius.* I feel so childish and self-absorbed.

"I'm so sorry."

Donnie leans his head back on my shoulder and tilts it toward me. I tangle our fingers together and wrap our arms around his stomach. I hold him, just hold him, letting him know I'm here, for whatever he needs.

"Do you want to talk about it?"

He takes a deep breath, then lets it out slowly. "It'll be four years. Sometimes it feels like yesterday. Sometimes it feels like it's been forever."

I don't know what that's like. I've never experienced anything even remotely similar. So I say nothing and wait.

"It was an accident. Roger was working late—again. He did that all the time. It was already dark by the time he left. He was always the worst at crossing streets. Always so preoccupied, thinking about a million things at once. He never checked for cars before stepping out onto the road. The taxi driver was going pretty fast and apparently a street lamp was out. Roger came out of nowhere and…"

Jesus Christ. My breath catches in my chest and my heart races as Donnie tells me the story. My entire body is braced like I'm the one about to get hit. I grip his hands hard and squeeze him tight. Even then, I'm shaking.

When I close my eyes, I can see the scene in my mind. The darkened street corner. Roger with his head down, lost in his own thoughts. The blare of the car horn. The screech of tires. And then… I force my eyes open. Yeah, having a cinematographic brain isn't always so fabulous.

"I was at Beau and Gavin's with a few other Mars people when the hospital called." Donnie's voice is eerily even. "He was in surgery when I got there, but they couldn't repair all the damage. They set him up in the ICU and he was awake for a bit."

He pauses and I hold my breath.

"I got to say goodbye."

As if that's any consolation for losing his husband.

My eyes prickle with tears and I try to fight them back. This moment isn't about me. It's about Donnie and I need to be strong for him. And yet, I'm struck by how fleeting life is. Here one minute, gone the next. No reason. No explanation. Shit happens and we just have to fucking live with it.

"I'm having lunch with Roger's parents tomorrow. We do it every year. We'll go to the cemetery together afterward."

"That's nice?" I say, more of a question than a comment. It's hard to tell exactly how Donnie's feeling when there's zero inflection in his voice.

"Sort of. It's… difficult."

I'm sure I have no idea how much.

Donnie tilts his head up to me. "Take me to bed?" he asks and my body kicks into gear.

Yes, I will absolutely take Donnie to bed. I will work him over and drive him so out of his mind that he can't think, never mind dwell on tomorrow. I will make him feel so good that the endorphins—or whatever brain chemical, he explained once but I can't remember—will carry him through lunch and all the way back home.

We go up to my room and slowly strip each other of our clothes. Donnie lays down on his back and I settle in between his thighs. I love it here. His thick legs wrapped around my waist, his lithe body writhing underneath me. He is the sexiest man I've ever set my eyes on and the most caring person I've ever had the pleasure to know.

I kiss him and he moans into my mouth. I drink up every last drop of it, licking his tongue, sucking it. His nails are scoring patterns across my back, lighting up my nerve endings until I'm quaking and quivering under his touch.

My dick is hard and as our bodies come together, it slips under his balls and rubs along his taint. It catches on the rim of his hole and it hits me how much I want to slide in there without a condom on. Nothing separating us. Nothing keeping us apart.

Soon. Get tested. Then we can ditch the condoms.

Donnie tilts his head back and I kiss my way along his stubbled jaw, down his neck to my absolute favorite spot right on top of his pulse. He's been sporting a hickey there for weeks and I make sure it's nice and purple every chance I get. He says the guys at Mars have been giving him shit for it. That only makes me suck on it harder.

I work my way down his body, my tongue retracing now-familiar paths across his chest. I sink my teeth into each ab muscle, left and right, left and right, all the way past his belly button to the base of his cock. Then I spend extra long minutes worshiping that sinful V.

It's the most sensitive spot Donnie has on his body—at least as far as I've been able to find. Nowhere else makes him squirm so hard or squeal so loud. I lap at them, soaking them in my saliva, ignoring the hard length of meat that lies between them. I don't let up until Donnie's begging for me, pleading for me to fuck him.

I push his legs up, knees to his chest, and dive into his ass. He tastes delectable—earthy and musky. I go a little wild whenever I get my tongue on him down there. He's a lot better at letting me in now than the first time we did this. Still, I take my time, licking into him over and over before adding my fingers into the mix. I don't want to hurt him, not tonight. I want everything to be smooth and silky and drag it out until we're both molasses.

"Connor." Donnie's hands are in my hair, tugging and scraping. "More."

I drizzle some lube onto my fingers and shift my mouth to his balls. They're so soft and delicate and the way they fill my mouth makes my groin tight with lust. I have to be careful with them, gentle with them. Donnie's letting me hold something so precious and I treat them with all the loving tenderness they deserve.

I let Donnie's balls drop out of my mouth and lick a stripe up the underside of his dick. Then I time it so my finger presses into him as his cock slides to the back of my mouth. Donnie lets out a whine that makes my dick leak. High and needy and I was the one who wrung it out of him. *I* did that. Me.

I suck his cock and fuck his ass, in and out and up and down, until Donnie's shouting my name and pleading with me to stick my dick in him. That's where I want him. That's where I want to keep him. I roll a condom on and notch my dick against the fluttering muscles of his hole. I lean forward to catch his mouth, then ease my way in.

It's staggering how perfect it is to be inside him. It's not just cock in ass. It feels like I'm somehow slotting into place with him. Like he's carved out a piece of himself, shaped especially for me. I'm safe here. I'm wanted here. Nothing can hurt me. I belong here.

I want to crawl deeper into him. I want to stay with him forever.

His ass muscles ripple around me and it sends a surge of pleasure through me. Donnie's unbelievable control over his body somehow extends down there too. I barely have to do anything if I don't want to. I can just bury myself in him and let his ass muscles milk every drop of cum from my balls.

Donnie kisses me, slow and deep, exploring every inch of my mouth like he's claiming it for himself. He's welcome to it. He can have my mouth, my cock, any and everything he wants of me. I'll give it to him. Willingly. Happily. His nails draw down to my ass and dig in hard.

"Come on, Connor. Fuck me," he murmurs against my lips. I can't say no.

I move and we both gasp at how good it feels. Our bodies come together and it's so beautiful that I get tears in my eyes sometimes.

Like this time. Donnie's all wrapped up around me. I've got my arms tucked under his body. We're rolling against each other, slick skin on slick skin. My forehead is pressed to his and we're breathing the same air. His cock is leaking a mess, sandwiched between our stomachs.

"Connor!"

He's getting close. I can tell by the way his muscles start quivering, the way his ass tightens around me. I reach between us for his dick, so hard and hot it burns my palm. I jerk him and fuck him and kiss him and then he's spilling his cum all over my hand. His ass clamps down on me like a fucking vise and I'm coming too, hips jerking to get as deep inside him as I can.

It's overwhelming. It's all-consuming. It rocks me in the innermost part of my soul. Every time we come together like this it feels like I lose a little piece of myself to Donnie. And that fills me with so much joy.

DONNIE

I stop a few feet away from the restaurant door to take a couple long, slow breaths. My heart rate is elevated and my breathing is too shallow. Connor was lovely yesterday, holding me on the couch, listening to me, then taking me upstairs to bed. I spent the night in his room, which I don't usually do. But I needed him with me and I didn't want to wake up alone.

Phyllis and Leonard are already waiting for me inside the restaurant. Four years on and this is still so hard. I thought it would get easier as time passed, but in some ways, it's getting more difficult.

I love Phyllis and Leonard. They're the parents I never had. Since the very first day I met them, they've been nothing but caring and supportive. They welcomed me into their family and treated me like their own son. Roger was really close to them his whole life. Before he died, we used to see them at least once a month.

Now, I see them maybe three times a year.

I pull out my phone and send Connor a text.

DONNIE

> At the restaurant now. I'll let you know when I'm on my way home.

Connor responds immediately with a series of hearts and thumbs-up emojis.

I plaster a smile onto my face and pull open the door. Phyllis sees me the minute I step inside and stands up to wave me over. I give them both long, tight hugs that I don't want to end.

Sadness wells up in me at seeing them again. I've missed them a lot, more than I've realized. They've always been so easy to be with. They've known me for so long that there's a deep familiarity between us that only comes with time. Sitting down with them now feels like coming home in a way I haven't felt since the last time I saw them.

It also hurts to see them though. We are the three people Roger loved the most while he was alive. We are the three people who loved him the most too. No matter who we talk to or how well we try to explain it, no one else in the entire world will understand exactly what it feels like to have loved him and lost him. We're bound together not merely by our shared love of Roger, but also by our shared pain. It's impossible to forget that when I see them.

"We ordered wine already. I hope that's okay." Phyllis lifts her glass in a silent salute and takes a sip.

"Would you like a glass?" Leonard picks up the bottle.

They know I don't drink much. I never have—except for maybe a two-week period when I tried to drown my sorrows and ended up on the bathroom floor more times than I'd like to admit. I drink even less now.

"No, thank you."

Leonard tops up Phyllis's glass instead.

"How are you, dear?" Phyllis asked. "You look good."

She's lying. I look like crap. I woke up halfway through the night, all tangled up with Connor in bed, with a sudden panic about what I was going to say to them at lunch. I crawled out of bed at first light, feeling like I've been punched in both eyes and I have the bruises to prove it.

I force my lips into a smile. "I'm okay."

It's an understatement and that's kind of the problem. The past few weeks with Connor have been wonderful. The shared meals, easy conversation, casual kisses, and heated touches. Movie nights and trips out into the city, sweet messages waiting for me on my phone after classes.

I've been smiling more than I have in ages. My steps feel lighter and the sun feels brighter. I have that giddy, walking on the clouds, everything is perfect feeling that comes at the beginning of every relationship. I haven't felt that in literal decades and my body and soul have been gorging on it.

Phyllis looks at me and I swear she can see inside my brain and read every single one of my thoughts. She gives me a smile that makes my eyes sting with tears and suddenly, I feel like an eight-year-old boy who wants his mother, rather than a fully grown man in his forties.

"That's wonderful. I'm so happy to hear that."

I switch the subject before I actually start crying in the middle of the restaurant. "How have you both been?"

"Oh, you know." Phyllis gives a dismissive wave of her hand. "We're the same."

"That's not true." Leonard reaches for his wife's hand. "We've started dance classes."

Phyllis blushes a dainty pink and Leonard gazes at her like they've just run off and eloped. It makes my heart ache to see that look in Leonard's eyes. It's the same way Roger used to look at me.

"What, um, what kind of dancing?" I ask.

"Latin ballroom," Phyllis says with a saucy shimmy of her shoulders. "Our neighbors coerced us into going with them."

"It's been fun," Leonard adds. "I've even shed a couple pounds." He pats his rounded stomach.

The waiter comes by to take our orders and refill our water glasses.

Leonard continues after he leaves. "Phyllis also has a new book club."

She giggles and leans toward me, bringing her hand up to cup her mouth. "It's not really a book club," she whispers. "It's a poker club. A bunch of us old ladies betting with pennies. But we call it a book club so we don't scandalize people."

I smile and it isn't forced this time. This time, I mean it from the depths of my heart. Dance classes and poker clubs. They're doing things that make them happy, that bring joy into their lives. They're living again and… I guess, so am I.

"Roger had regular poker nights with friends, didn't he?" Phyllis has a faraway look in her eyes.

My heart clenches, bracing itself for what's coming. This is why lunch with Phyllis and Leonard can be so difficult. The reminiscing. I have zero problems with talking about Roger. I'm more than happy to answer every question Connor might have about him.

It's different with Phyllis and Leonard though. It's the back and forth. My emotions fuel their emotions, which fuel mine again until it becomes too much. Then I'm suddenly back there, in the days after we lost him, rocked with the realization that he's gone and he's never coming back.

"Yeah," I say, my voice tight and a little too high. "He did. Once a month with his work friends. He wasn't very good at it though. He had the worst poker face I've ever seen."

Leonard shakes his head, smiling at a private memory. "He never could lie to us."

"It was in his eyes," Phyllis adds. "We could always tell by the look in his eyes. He was such a sweet child."

The waiter comes by with our plates and I poke at my grilled fish.

That sweet child grew up into a sweet man. One who called his mother every other day, who brought home flowers on Fridays, who lit up every room he walked into. He used to drive out to Long Island to spend an afternoon with his father doing yard work. He paid for the four of us to go on a cruise together once.

I shift in my chair, fighting the itch to get up and walk out for some air. I pick up my glass of water instead and down half of it.

God, I miss him so much sometimes. I miss having him move in the same space as me. I miss his smell. I miss knowing what he's thinking without having to ask. I miss finishing his sentences for him and having him finish mine.

I even miss all the things he was shite at, too. That cruise we all went on? He spent the first three days sequestered in the business center for work. Yard work in Long Island was fine, but try getting him to lift a finger with our own backyard. Good luck. I miss all the ways he annoyed me because they were a part of who he was. He wouldn't have been Roger without them.

Phyllis's hand settles over mine on the table. I glance up to find her watching me, a knowing look in her eyes.

"I miss him too, dear."

I nod, my heart in my throat.

She tilts her head to the side and narrows her eyes a fraction. "Have you started dating yet?"

My eyes bulge out of my head and I choke on my own saliva. I grab for my water and bang on my chest, more as a stalling tactic than anything else. This was what kept me up all night. Whether I should tell them about Connor.

"Are you all right, dear?"

"Yes, sorry, I just..." I suck in a deep breath. "You caught me off-guard."

"So is that a yes? You've started dating?" Phyllis asks again.

"Phyllis, we don't need to go prying into Donnie's life."

"It's not prying." She shoots him a glare. "I'm just looking out for our son's best interests."

I freeze and my eyes snap to Phyllis, but she's still glaring at Leonard. It probably just slipped out. Or she meant "son" in a figurative sense because I used to be her son-in-law. Yes, we considered ourselves family once, but that was before, and I barely ever see them these days. They couldn't possibly…

Except Leonard's studying me and I feel like I've been caught breaking curfew or something.

"Actually, this might be a good time to mention…" He glances at Phyllis with a questioning look.

"Oh, yes, that."

That what?

Leonard stares me right in the eyes. "We've changed our will so that everything goes to you once we're gone."

I don't understand right away. Why would they do that?

"It's not going to be billions or anything," Phyllis says, with an exaggerated hand wave. "But there will be a good chunk left. And the house, of course."

"What?" My voice is small with my heart lodged right up there in my throat.

Phyllis and Leonard exchange a look, then she smiles at me with so much tender indulgence that I can't breathe.

"Donnie, you're our son. It makes sense for us to put you in our will."

"But… but…" I don't have the words to describe this mix of indebtedness and unworthiness and humility churning inside me. They don't owe me anything. I haven't done anything to deserve a gesture like that. I came here today debating whether I should tell them that I'm sleeping with someone who isn't their son.

"My dear, you became our son the day you and Roger became partners. That hasn't changed just because Roger isn't with us anymore."

"But…"

Phyllis tsks at me. "No buts, you hear me? We're family."

The tears slip past my lashes and I swipe at them, trying not to draw attention to myself. Hearing Phyllis call us family is like the prickling sensation when feeling returns to a limb that's gone numb. It hurts like fucking hell, but it's life coming back to a part of me that I'd forgotten was there.

I've been so lonely and I'd resigned myself to that solitary existence. Connor somehow wormed his way in and set up camp inside me. And now Phyllis and Leonard are reminding me of how much I've pushed away the people who love me most. Maybe it was what I needed at the time, to lick my wounds by myself. But I need life now. I need to live.

"You've been alone for too long," Phyllis says, like she's plucking my thoughts straight out of my brain. "You need to start seeing people."

I nod. She's right. "I have been seeing someone," I manage to whisper.

Phyllis's face lights up. "I knew it!" She looks so excited and eager that I have to laugh.

It's a laugh that breaks through that dark, heavy place inside me. It shakes something loose, like a chunk of rock falling away from me. My body feels lighter. It's easier to breathe. My heart rate settles closer to its resting pace.

"Tell me about him?" Phyllis asks, like we're teenagers gossiping about boys.

I smile at the thought of him, the boy who is changing my life. "His name is Connor."

DONNIE

After lunch, I follow Leonard and Phyllis to the cemetery in the car Roger and I shared. I don't use it often. I don't like driving very much and there really isn't a need for it in the city. But during times like this, when I need to go to an out-of-the-way place, it's nice to have.

The air is thick when I step out of the car. Gray clouds rolled in during the drive to the restaurant, hanging low and heavy in the sky. I feel like I'm walking through water. Every breath feels like I'm sucking in steam.

It's always kind of a surreal experience when I visit the cemetery. I don't fully feel like myself. Almost like I'm outside of my body, watching it weave through the headstones with a bouquet in its hand. My skin feels tingly and numb at the same time. My insides feel hollow.

It's the same today—but worse. I told Phyllis and Leonard all about Connor over lunch. They asked dozens of questions. They want to meet him. I got that little tickle of nervousness at the prospect of introducing the boy I'm dating to my parents. I want them to like him. I want him to like them.

Most importantly, they're supportive of me dating someone new and that was what had me up all night. I've gotten their blessing and now I'm at Roger's plot looking for… permission, absolution, something.

I'm afraid I won't find what I'm looking for. The fear sits in the middle of my chest, its talons sunk deep into me. I've lived with this grief for so long, it's become a part of me. I don't know how to let it go or who I am without it.

But I don't want to move forward with Connor still carrying this soul-deep sense of loss. He doesn't deserve to have this heavy mantle sitting on top of the relationship we're trying to build. It'll be doomed before it even starts if I don't do something about it now.

So I'm here, heart in my throat, gut sickeningly empty, knowing that it's all up to me, but not sure if I'm strong enough to do it.

I hang back to let Phyllis and Leonard approach Roger's headstone by themselves. He has his arm around her and she leans her head on his shoulder. It's beautiful seeing them stand there, side-by-side, after so many years together. It's heartbreaking that they're standing in front of their son's grave.

I send up a silent promise to Roger. *I'll take care of them. For the rest of their lives, no matter what happens, I'll be there for them the way you would've been.* The promise sinks into me, into that deep, dark place, and wedges itself between the boulders I've collected there. It's pushing them apart, jimmying them loose.

Phyllis and Leonard pull away from each other and

turn to me. Leonard's sniffling. Phyllis is wiping her cheeks. They're both smiling at me.

"Come here, Donnie." Phyllis waves me over.

I come crashing back into my body in that moment. Blood rushes past my ears as my heart hammers against my ribs. My guts are twisted into knots so tight it's almost physically painful. The fear is squeezing my chest until I can't breathe.

Phyllis drags me forward and they sandwich me between them. I bend stiffly to set my flowers next to theirs and when I stand up, they both take each of my hands. We form a little circle with Roger's headstone taking up the fourth side.

"We're family," Phyllis says, giving my hand a little shake by our sides. "Me and Leonard and Roger and you. Nothing's ever going to change that."

I nod, trying to hold off the tears for as long as I can.

"Roger loved you so much. And we do too. He would never want you to be alone for the rest of your life, Donnie. And we don't either."

The tears come, hot and fast, and I let them run down my face and land on the grass at my feet.

"He would want you to be happy, to love again, to have all the things you had with him."

Every word Phyllis speaks is a wrecking ball against the mountain of rocks I've built inside, on top of, and around me. Fractures are forming in the barrier I've constructed to keep myself safe. It hurts. Oh god, it hurts, but I can't go back anymore. I can't keep living under this burden. I can only move forward.

"This Connor? Your Connor?" Phyllis keeps going. "He sounds really wonderful, my dear."

Another swing of the wrecking ball, and another crack ruptures through me. It's in a spot that's already been weakened by bits of Connor that have worked their way into me over the past few weeks. They're all over the place, I realize.

Every laugh, every smile. Every time we've teased each other and every time we've come together in bed. They're all little seeds that have wound deeper and deeper into me in preparation for this moment.

"I hope we get to meet him soon. I need to make sure he's good enough for my son." Phyllis nudges me with her elbow and something that's halfway between a laugh and a sob bursts out of me.

She pulls me into a fierce hug. "We love you, Donnie. We want only the best for you."

"I love you too," I say through my tears.

Phyllis steps away and Leonard takes her place. He gives me a couple strong slaps on the back and murmurs his own, "I love you."

A drop of water lands on the side of my face as he lets me go. Thunder rumbles low and menacing across the sky. The clouds have gotten darker, casting everything in shadow.

"You should go," I say, moving Phyllis into Leonard's arms. None of us have umbrellas. "You don't want to get caught in the rain."

"You're not coming?" Phyllis asks.

I shake my head and manage to give her a genuine smile. "I need a few more minutes on my own. You go ahead. Have a safe drive home."

They turn toward their car and I wait until they've climbed inside.

A drop of rain lands on my nose, then another on Roger's headstone, turning the dusty gray almost black. I crouch down so I'm level with the engraving and trace my fingers along Roger's name.

"I miss you. So much."

Fat, heavy drops land all around me like a leaky faucet.

"Some days I wake up and it hits me all over again. I'm never going to hear the way you laugh anymore. I'm never going to feel your arms around me. Your pillow is never going to smell like you again."

My tears are flowing steadily now and the rain is matching my pace. Water trails down the back of my neck and wets my collar. My hair is plastered to my head. I put my hand flat against the smooth face of the headstone and collapse to my knees in the soggy grass.

"It's better now with Connor. I haven't had as many of those moments since I met him."

In the distance, lightning flashes and thunder rolls.

"He makes me laugh, kind of the way you used to make me laugh. He lights up the room the way you used to too. It's nice having him in the house. It doesn't echo so much when he's there."

Lightning flashes again, closer this time. The thunder is louder too. It rumbles through me and the rocks start tumbling off. I sob. I can't help it. I'm breaking apart and the rain is washing it all away. The tears on my face. The crumbling rubble inside. I let it all go and tilt my head back to look up at the sky.

The rain is cold and stings my heated forehead and cheeks. I sit like that for long moments, not caring that I'm soaked through, not caring that my pants are ruined. My tears slow and the thick heavy walls I've hidden behind all these years are little more than ruins. I drop my head forward, hands digging into the wet grass in front of me.

"Your mom said it was okay for me to move on. She said you'd want me to find someone new. I know she's right. I know that's what you want."

The rain lets up a tiny bit, the sheets easing back into individual drops. There's a calmness inside me that I haven't felt in a long time. It's quiet and peaceful and still.

"He's young, you know," I whisper to Roger's headstone with a smile. "So eager, driven, hard on himself. I think you would've liked him. I think you two would've been friends."

The rain stops. There's one last little rumble of thunder, but it's far away now. The air smells earthy and clean. I breathe it in and fill myself up with it.

"You're not going to believe this. He's a filmmaker. He's making me watch movies. We're working our way up to the scary ones. You know how much I hate scary movies. But we're getting lots of use out of that theater room you insisted we put in."

The clouds lift into the sky and thin out until they're nothing but wisps. A single ray of sunshine breaks through.

"Yeah," I laugh. "I thought you'd like that."

The sunshine is warm on my face and the sky is shockingly blue. I lean forward and press my forehead to the cold, wet stone.

I'm drained but I feel light. My heart is tender but it's whole. Roger isn't here anymore but he'll always be with me.

I press a kiss to his name. "I love you."

CONNOR

"Donnie! I'm home!" I drop my bag by the foot of the stairs and head to the kitchen to find him.

He was nervous this morning before I left for work, on edge about seeing Roger's parents and visiting the cemetery. I pushed him against the counter and got down on my knees in the kitchen to give him a breakfast blowjob before rushing out the door.

He messaged in the late afternoon to tell me he was heading home from the cemetery, so he should be in full-scale cooking mode by now. But there's no one in the kitchen. "Donnie?"

I spin around and poke my head down the stairs into the basement. Nothing. He's not in my bedroom. I peek quickly into Roger's office, just in case. Nope. Not there either.

I hesitate before climbing the stairs to the third floor. I've only been up there once or twice. I kinda think of it as Donnie's domain. Donnie and Roger's domain. Plus, we don't really have a reason to sleep in his bed when mine is usually closer.

"Donnie?" I call up. No response.

Maybe he went back out? Maybe he's taking a nap. But no, something feels off, and I don't like it. I climb the steps. The door to the bedroom is closed, so I give it a gentle knock before cracking it open.

There's a Donnie-shaped lump on the bed and my heart clenches at the sight. The visit probably took a lot out of him. He did warn me that might happen. But he does look awfully still…

I slip inside, close the door behind me with a snick, and tiptoe up to the bed. I'm just going to check that he's okay. Maybe crawl in beside him and hold him until he wakes up. I peer over the blankets and see his face.

Donnie is not okay.

His eyes are sunken in and his skin is pale with bright red splotches on his cheeks. His hair is soaked through with sweat and he's shivering despite the thick covers he's under. I reach for his forehead and I can feel the heat radiating off him before my hand even makes contact.

"Shit."

Donnie stirs at my touch, groaning and grimacing, but he doesn't open his eyes.

"Donnie?" My heart races and my brain starts throwing out worst-case scenarios. Do I need to call for an ambulance and go with him to the hospital? What if it's something more serious than a cold or the flu?

"Shit, shit, shit."

I fumble for my phone and step on something wet. It looks like the clothes Donnie was wearing this morning, drenched and in a pile on the floor. *What the—whatever.* I'll deal with it later.

I stare at my phone. What do I do? What do I do?

I pull up the phone number of the only person I can think of to call. "Come on, come on. Pick up, pick up."

"Hello?"

"Mom, what do I do if someone has a fever?" I pace away from the bed, one hand tugging at my hair, the slight pain keeping me from spinning completely out of control.

"What? Who has a fever? Are you okay?"

"I'm fine. It's not me."

"Is it Miles? Wyatt?"

I drop into the winged back armchair by the window and lean forward to brace my elbows on my knees. "No, Mom, it's not either of them," I say, gritting my teeth. "You don't know him, okay? Just tell me what to do when someone has a fever!"

"There's no need to use that tone of voice with me, young man."

"Mom!" I almost yell.

She huffs a sigh. "How high is his temperature?"

I rush back to Donnie's side and press my hand to his forehead. "I don't know. It's high."

I can practically hear her rolling her eyes. "How high? Do you have a thermometer?"

"No, I don't." But maybe Donnie does. "Hold on, lemme see if I can find one."

I throw open Donnie's door and hesitate. Where do people keep thermometers? Bathrooms? I hurry down the hall to Donnie's.

"Gimme a sec, I'm looking." I set my phone down on the counter and start rummaging through the medicine cabinet. Razor, cologne, face wash, moisturizer. No ther-mometer.

"Come on, Donnie, where's your thermometer? Where would you keep a thermometer?" I drop down to check the cabinet under the sink. In the corner is a white box with a big red cross on it. I toss out stacks of band-aids and gauze and wipes before I find the digital thermometer at the bottom. I press the on button—*please work, please work*—and the old-school digital display flickers to life. "Thank-fucking-god."

I pick up the phone again. "Mom? I found it."

"There's no need to swear, Connor."

"Oh my god, Mom, please."

"Please, what? Go take his temperature."

Donnie is in the exact same position I left him in, curled up on his side, face half buried in a pillow. I can't just jab the thing into his mouth, can I? "He's asleep. What do I do?"

"You can wake him up," she says, like it's the most obvious thing in the world.

I cringe. "Are you sure? Shouldn't I let him rest?"

"Fine, then don't wake him up."

"But then, how do I know what his temperature is?" My voice is squeaky, my skin is prickly, and my heart is trying to beat its way out of my chest. If Donnie is really sick, if he needs to go to the hospital… I don't know how to do any of that stuff. I don't know how to take care of him the way he took care of me.

"Connor, breathe. It's going to be okay."

"How do you know that? You don't know that."

"Connor, stop it." Her voice is steely and sharp.

I snap my mouth shut.

"You're going to let him rest and when he wakes up, you'll take his temperature. What's his name?"

"Huh?" What does Donnie's name have to do with his temperature?

"The person who's sick. What is his name?"

"Uh, Donnie?" I don't know why I said it like I wasn't sure what it was.

"Donnie? That's his name?"

"Yes, Donnie."

"Okay, if Donnie's temperature is above one-hundred-and-four, then take him to the hospital."

"Wait, wait. I need to write this down." I switch her to speaker phone and pull up my notes app. "When should I take him to the hospital?"

"If his temperature is above one-hundred-and-four."

"And how do I get him there?"

There's a beat of silence before she speaks, voice resigned. "Don't worry about that right now."

"Okay, okay, I can do that. What else?"

"You can give him acetaminophen or ibuprofen. Just follow the instructions on the bottle."

"Instructions on the bottle, okay." My fingers tremble as I try to type on my phone. Why won't autocorrect work when I goddamn need it to work?

"If he's sweating, he'll need lots of fluids to make up for it."

"He is. He's sweating a lot."

"You might need to help him shower, if he's up for it. Then clean, dry clothes and clean, dry linens. Make sure he stays warm. Sometimes a cool towel on the forehead feels nice."

"Shower. Clothes. Linens. Cool towel on forehead. Okay, anything else?"

"That's it. If the fever doesn't break within a couple days, you might need to take him to the hospital. But we'll deal with that when the time comes."

"Yeah, okay. Maybe it'll break before then."

"Connor, are you okay?" Her voice is softer now. She's not asking about the fever.

I squeeze my eyes shut, feeling like an idiot. Twenty-fucking-six years old and calling my mommy because I've never taken care of someone with a fever before. Roger would've known what to do.

"Yeah, I think so."

She sighs, sending a rush of air over the phone's mic. "All right, well, call me again if you need anything else."

I nod. "Okay, I will. Thanks, Mom."

We hang up and I take a couple deep breaths. I need to calm the fuck down. Donnie needs me.

He isn't dying. He probably just got caught in that freak rainstorm earlier. That would explain the pile of wet clothes on the floor. He's going to be fine. And even if he gets worse, even if I have to take him to the hospital… one thing at a time. I have to focus on right now.

Mom said fluids, clean clothes, and clean linens. I go downstairs and dig out the Gatorades Donnie always has stocked in the fridge. If electrolytes are good for hydrating after a workout, they have to be good for hydrating after a fever, right? Feels like the same principle to me. I line up the bottles on the nightstand and go to the walk-in closet.

I flick the light on and take a half-step back. Damn, this walk-in closet is bigger than some New York apartments I've been in. Clothes hang in neat rows. Shoes are on display in a column of shelves. Bags line the shelves near the ceiling. One side of the closet has more athletic wear than any one person should own. The other side is filled with suits. Expensive-looking suits.

Donnie said he still has a lot of Roger's clothes. I didn't realize that "a lot" means all of them. I move toward that side of the closet and run my hands along the shoulders of the jackets. The hangers are all evenly spaced out.

Roger feels bigger than life in my head. Smart, charming, self-assured, sweet. He worked on Wall Street at a high-profile job that raked in piles of cash, so much that Donnie's got more than enough to live off of now. He hosted fancy dinner parties. He wore brand names that I've never even heard of. He renovated old houses in New York until they looked like magazine spreads.

Me? I'm calling my mom because I got freaked out by a fever. I rub my eyes with the heels of my hands, then run my fingers through my hair. It doesn't feel nearly as good as when Donnie does it.

I need to pull myself together and be the adult that Donnie needs me to be. Not just today, not just to nurse him back to health. Roger left big shoes to fill, and I'm not saying I'll ever be able to fill them completely, but he was someone Donnie could depend on. He was a partner to Donnie. I need to be that—someone Donnie can depend on, someone he can partner with.

There's a stack of linens and bedding in the corner and I grab a set. A quick check of the drawers reveals Donnie's stash of PJs. I bring them all into the bedroom right as Donnie groans.

"Connor?"

I dump all the neatly folded fabric on the armchair and

rush to his side. He's flung the covers off, thrashing around with a grimace on his face.

"Hey, I'm here."

He groans and rolls toward me, flinging his arm in my direction. His eyes are screwed shut. I don't think he's awake.

"It's okay."

I brush the damp hair off his forehead. "What's okay?"

"Roger says it's okay."

My breath catches in my chest. What—did he—no, he's dreaming. He's definitely dreaming. He didn't somehow read my mind, confer with his late husband, and then come back to reassure me that I don't need to measure myself against Roger. We're not in a movie. Donnie is not Whoopi Goldberg.

"Donnie, wake up." I give him a little shake, but he rolls onto his other side.

His entire back is wet with sweat and so are the sheets he's lying on. He shivers and doesn't stop. I'll have to wait until he wakes up to help him change, but in the meantime, I pull the covers over him and tuck them around his body.

Donnie sighs in his sleep. I lay down next to him, scooting in as close as I can with the blankets between us. I gently rest my hand on his side, measuring the rise and fall of his breathing, each one a sign that he's going to be okay.

I wish I could've known Roger: the person Donnie fell in love with, the person he built a life with. Donnie wouldn't be who he is today if it wasn't for Roger. If it wasn't for Roger, I wouldn't have this chance to know Donnie, to live in this house, to love him.

My heart somersaults in my chest.

I love Donnie.

I take a breath and poke at the feeling inside me. I'm pretty sure it's love. I've never felt it before, not like this. It has to be love, right?

I like how it feels. Big and strong, yet delicate and soft. I feel like I can conquer anything with it and I feel extremely vulnerable at the same time. It has to be love.

Donnie shifts toward me in his sleep. I arrange myself the best I can with all the blankets. It kinda feels like I'm hugging a furnace. There's nowhere else I would rather be.

DONNIE

My mouth tastes like arse. Not the good kind of arse. The bad kind where every breath makes me want to gag.

I hurt everywhere. From the hair follicles in my scalp to the tips of my toes, there isn't a single inch of flesh in my body that doesn't ache and protest when I move. Not that I can move. I'm trapped under what feels like two tons of blankets.

The room is mostly dark when I try to open my eyes. Connor is curled up next to me, *on top* of the blankets, one arm flung over me and the other hand tucked under the pillow by his cheek.

He looks so peaceful when he's sleeping, with the bottom lip tucked under his top one like he's sucking on it. I've watched him sleep before, usually in the middle of the night before I untangle myself from his bed and come back upstairs to mine. Except this time—I glance around quickly without daring to move my head—we're in my bedroom, not his.

My eyes slide shut. I had lunch with Phyllis and Leonard, then we visited Roger at the cemetery. I sat in the rain and got soaked to the bone. By the time I got home, I felt like shite and had laid down to take a nap. Connor must have found me like this. How long ago was that? What time is it?

I try to get my arm out of the blanket cocoon I'm trapped in and the movement wakes Connor up. He blinks, rubs his eyes, and makes an adorable sleepy sound.

"Hey, you're awake."

"I kind of wish I wasn't." My mouth is gross and my bladder is screaming at me, but the rest of me wants to sink back into unconscious oblivion.

"How do you feel?"

"Like I got run over by a train."

Connor chuckles and swings himself off the bed. Just watching him move so easily, so smoothly, makes my body hurt.

"You kinda look like it too."

"Gee, thanks."

He leans over the bed, holding an ancient digital thermometer. "Put this under your tongue. I need to take your temperature."

I don't need a thermometer to know I have a fever and it's running high. Still, I open my mouth and let him stick the pointy end in. "Where'd you find this thing?" I mumble around it.

"In the first aid kit in your bathroom."

"Hmm." I don't even remember having a thermometer. I can't remember the last time I was sick enough to need one.

It beeps and Connor pulls it out of my mouth. "One-hundred-and-two. Not great but I don't need to take you to the hospital yet."

I groan and close my eyes. "No, no hospital. I just need rest. I'll be fine."

There's a muted cracking sound and when I open my eyes, Connor's holding a bottle of Gatorade in front of me. "You've been sweating buckets. You need to hydrate." There's a hint of glee when he says that last word.

He's right, except drinking requires moving and moving hurts.

"Come on. Let me help you." Connor sets the bottle down and pushes some of the blankets off me.

I gasp at the blast of cold air and my entire body throbs like I'm one giant heartbeat. Connor settles me against the headboard, propped up with pillows, and hands me the Gatorade.

I take it with both hands, even though I can't really feel them. My fingers, my arms, my shoulders, none of them really feel connected to my brain. It's like my body is a puppet and I control their movements, but they don't really belong to me.

The Gatorade is heavenly, masking the taste of arse in my mouth and soothing the fire inside me. I drink down as much as I can until my stomach can't take anymore. It gurgles. I'm starving.

"What time is it?"

Connor checks his phone. "Almost six in the morning."

No wonder my stomach feels so hollow. I slept right through dinner and straight into the next day. "Did you eat last night?" I ask Connor.

He bites his lip and shakes his head. "I was going to

stay with you for a bit and then go down to eat, but then I fell asleep."

I notice now that he's wearing the same clothes as yesterday. I feel awful. He shouldn't neglect himself just to take care of me.

"Are you hungry? I can heat up leftovers for you if you want." Connor takes the Gatorade bottle when I hand it back to him.

There isn't anything in the fridge I want to eat—not at almost six in the morning and not when I'm feeling half-dead.

"Or do you want to take a shower?" Connor asks. "I can change the bedsheets too."

That's a good idea. Except I'm not sure if I can make it two steps past the edge of the bed.

"Here, lemme help." He holds out his hand and I go to him.

I sigh when his hands touch my body, when his arms wrap around me and support my weight. I lean against him, like he's a healing balm and the more of him I get on me, the better I'll feel.

I float toward the bathroom, not feeling the floor under my feet, not feeling the legs under me. I'm cold. I hurt. I curl toward Connor who makes everything better.

"Whoa," he murmurs, staring at the jumble of knobs in the walk-in shower.

I point to the big one at the top of the column. "That one. Turn it about halfway to the left."

Connor leaves me leaning against the chilly wall and turns the water on. It comes pouring out of the rainwater showerhead with a loud splash. "And I thought the bathroom downstairs was fancy."

I grunt. "The other knobs are body jets."

Connor's kneeling in front of me, helping me out of my sweats. He looks up, eyes wide. "What are body jets?"

"Turn them on and find out."

Connor eyes me suspiciously and I laugh, only to groan at how much it hurts. He stands to help lift my t-shirt over my head. It's excruciating trying to lift my too-heavy arms above my head. But once I walk into the piping hot water, I moan at how good it feels.

I sway on my feet and reach for the closest wall for support. My knees are weak and my head is spinning. I wish I had a chair.

Then strong arms come around me and I sigh. Connor's wide and solid and warm, better than any chair, better than any wall. I turn into him and rest my head on his shoulder, letting him hold me up, trusting him not to let me fall.

"Turn on the body jets. The other knobs."

Connor shifts me to one side and reaches for them. It takes him a bit of fiddling and then water comes shooting out at us from jets hidden in the walls.

"Whoa! What!"

I smile against Connor's shoulder and finally stop shivering. Connor's hands run up and down my back. My dick stirs at his touch, at his naked, wet body pressed so close to mine. Connor pauses at the small of my back before venturing lower to grab my arse, gently massaging my glutes in his large palms.

I lift my head to brush my lips along his jaw, to rub my stubbled cheek against his smooth one. My hands come up to his hips and around to his lower back, and I let out a moan at the way Connor's chest and stomach slide deliciously over mine. He's hard too and when his cock juts against my hip, I dig my fingers into his back to keep him there.

"Fuck, Donnie." Connor's voice is strained. "You've got a fever."

"Hmm." I'm already burning up, what are a few more degrees? I grind my hips against his and nip at his ear.

"Fuck."

"S'okay." I turn in Connor's arms until we're back to chest and I adjust us so his cock is snug between my thighs. Christ, he feels so good back there, long and hard against my taint. I want to tell him that he belongs there, that we're meant to be together like this. Naked and raw, at our most vulnerable.

I want to tell him that I'm good now. I had a breakthrough. I'm ready to move forward and I want to move forward with him.

Connor pinches my nipple with one hand and wraps his fingers around my dick with the other. I gasp and melt back against him, head resting on his shoulder.

"Fuck me," I murmur into his ear. I need him. I need his mark on me. I need him to know that I'm his. I reach up for the back of his head and pull him down so his lips are on my neck, on that spot on my neck.

"Jesus Christ, Donnie." Connor seals his lips over his mark at the same time as his hand tightens around my cock. His hips snap forward, ramming into the back of my balls.

I latch onto his hip, to his scalp, digging my nails into him as he moves for the both of us. Water falls on my face, heavy drops splatter on my sensitive nipples. Connor sucks on the skin right above my collarbone and my whine echoes off the walls of the bathroom.

My balls ache where they're getting battered by Connor's dick. My cock throbs as Connor's hand flies over it. The pressure building in my groin is strong enough to obscure how the rest of my body hurts so bad. I whine again, the sound mingling with Connor's deep, rhythmic grunts.

"Donnie, I'm going to come."

"Hmm." *Yes, come for me, my darling.*

"Fuck, I'm coming. I'm coming."

Scalding hot cum paints my taint, the back of my balls, so much hotter than the water sluicing over us, so much hotter than the fever burning inside me. My stomach clenches, my thighs tense, my whole body goes taut as the orgasm incinerates me. Pleasure courses through me, flooding my nerve endings until I feel nothing but bliss.

No more aches. No more pain. No more shivering in the cold. I smile and collapse into Connor, all those wonderful endorphins and oxytocin working their magic in my body.

I nuzzle Connor's neck and float away.

CONNOR

Sex was most definitely not what I had in mind when I got in the shower with Donnie. He wasn't steady on his feet and the last thing I wanted was to add a concussion to his fever.

I kinda feel bad though, as I quickly soap him up and rinse him down. Did I just take advantage of him? He's a little dazed but he doesn't seem delirious or anything. I turn off the water and towel him off. He's soft and languid as I help him into clean pajamas and settle him into the armchair. He grabs my hand before I can go change the sheets.

"Thank you, Connor."

My heart somersaults and I press a kiss to his forehead. If he's thanking me for the orgasm, well, I'm coming out of that one a winner too, baby.

I strip the bed down in record time and wrestle a fresh fitted sheet over the mattress. When I turn back to Donnie, he's gazing at me with half-lidded eyes and a tiny grin on his lips.

I crouch down in front of him. "Hey."

"Hey."

"Feeling better after the shower?"

He nods and blinks slowly. My heart swells with so much affection and love for him, for this man who appeared out of nowhere, who helped hold me together when I was falling apart. He's strong and capable, but gentle and unguarded at the same time. I've never met anyone like him before and I'm pretty sure I never will.

I press another kiss to his forehead. It still burns hot under my lips, but Donnie doesn't look as wrecked as he did when I first found him. I get him back into bed, with fresh blankets tucked in around him.

I hold up another bottle of Gatorade and when he nods, I twist the cap off for him. "I'm gonna heat up something from the fridge."

Donnie scowls. "There should be canned soup in the pantry."

"*Canned* soup?" I over-exaggerate my surprise. "Since when do you eat canned soup?"

"Extenuating circumstances."

I laugh. "Okay. I'll go check. You'll be okay up here?"

He smiles sleepily at me. "I'll be fine."

I leave him sipping his Gatorade and go downstairs to find exactly two cans of minestrone soup in the pantry. I pour them both into a pot to heat up on the stove.

I can't cook nearly as well as Donnie can but I know the basics. Spaghetti with pasta sauce. Eggs, bacon, and toast. If Donnie has a slow cooker stashed around here somewhere, I can make chili from canned beans and tomatoes. I have no idea what to do with the eggplant, parsley, and cabbage I find in the fridge though.

There's a sleeve of crackers in the pantry and I put them on the tray along with our bowls of soup to bring up to Donnie. He's sitting exactly where I left him, propped up against the headboard, eyes closed, head lolling to one side. I set the tray down on the ottoman next to the armchair and gently shake Donnie awake.

He grimaces as he stretches his neck. "Sorry, I fell asleep."

"You're supposed to be sleeping. I'm sorry I took so long." I bring him his bowl and make sure he's got a good grip on it before I let go.

"Thank you. Smells amazing."

I snort, even as warmth spreads through me. "It's canned soup. I just heated it up."

Donnie takes a sip and lets out a quiet sigh. The look of calm contentment on his face makes me want to scoop him up and hold him in my lap. I'm so incredibly lucky that he was at Mars that night. Who knows where I'd be right now if he hadn't been there to catch me when I fell?

I bring my own bowl of soup to the bed and sit at his feet. He lifts his spoon to his lips again and my eyes latch onto the pale band of skin around his ring finger. I gasp silently and stare. He's taken off his wedding ring. When did he do that?

"How, uh…" I force myself to take a sip of soup and slow myself down. "How was lunch and stuff yesterday?"

Donnie looks at his hand too, and he doesn't answer right away. When he lifts his gaze to mine, I'm hit by the depth of emotion in his eyes. There's still a hint of grief and sadness—the little piece of Roger that he'll always carry around with him. But there's so much peace, so much joy, and so much affection. It's all aimed at me.

"It went well."

I drag in a breath, taking in all the feelings Donnie's directing toward me. They fill me up, seeping into all my nooks and crannies, until I feel like I'm going to explode with happiness.

"Tell me?"

"Phyllis and Leonard want to meet you."

My eyes bulge. "You told them about me?"

Donnie nods slowly, then stills. "I told Roger about you too. I mean… at the cemetery."

I swallow down my emotions so I can speak. "And?"

Donnie smiles again, with all that peace and joy and affection. "I think he would have liked you."

Oh god, my heart is so full. "I think I would've liked him too."

Donnie rubs his thumb across his bare ring finger. It's the same gesture he did when he played with the ring. "It was time."

I nod.

When he reaches his hand to me, I take it and bring it to my lips. I hold it there. *If you're listening, Roger, I promise to take care of him. You can trust him with me.*

We finish eating and I make sure Donnie's all tucked into bed, with his phone close by in case he needs to reach me. I take the tray back downstairs and head out to the grocery store. If we want to eat anything besides takeout for the next couple days, I need stuff I actually know how to cook.

It's sunny when I step outside. The sky is blue and spotted with those fluffy white clouds. It's one of those days when everything is perfect and nothing can go wrong. When strangers smile as we pass each other on the sidewalk, and puppies run up to me for head scritches.

I pull my phone out as I walk and dial the number for Mars. Sawyer answers.

"Hey Sawyer, it's Connor." Sawyer and I have chatted more every time I've been at Mars. He's a cool guy, getting his bachelor's degree part-time while he works at the gym.

"Hey, Connor! What's up? How's it going?"

Things are going freaking great. I'm in love with Donnie and he took his wedding ring off and I might be the happiest I've ever been in my entire life. I don't say any of that.

"Actually, I'm calling because Donnie's caught a cold or the flu or something."

"Oh, shit. Is he okay?"

"I think so. He just needs to rest. So he's not gonna make it to his classes for the next couple days."

"Yeah, yeah, cool. No prob. I'll let Beau and Gavin know. We can find someone to cover for him."

I can hear Sawyer shuffling things around on the other end of the line. "Thanks. I'll have Donnie reach out when he's feeling better."

"Awesome! I hope he gets better soon!"

I hang up and send a message to Rick.

CONNOR

> Hey Rick, since we don't have any shoots lined up for this week, is it okay if I work from home? My

I stop walking. What exactly do I call Donnie? I want to say boyfriend, but am I allowed to do that yet?

roomie is sick and I'd like to stay with him.

I can't imagine why Rick would say no, so I slip my phone back into my pocket and lift my face toward the sky. When Donnie gets better, we should go to the park. We can have a picnic and then catch one of those free movies they play in the summer. I'll need to check the schedule for those. We should go cycling too. I wanna ride behind him so I can watch those thighs and ass in action.

I grab a basket at the fancy grocery store Donnie likes to shop at. I'm more of a Trader Joe's guy myself, but Donnie's place is closer to home. I head straight for the canned goods aisle and stock up on chicken soup, beef stew, and a few different kinds of beans and crushed tomatoes. A box of spaghetti and a jar of sauce from the pasta aisle. I swing through the fruit section, picking up bananas, navel oranges, and grapes, because I think Donnie will try to revolt if I don't give him at least a couple healthy options.

I balk when the cashier tells me the total, but I hand over my credit card anyway. It's fine. It's for Donnie. It's worth it.

With my arms full of groceries, I don't notice until it's almost too late. One second, I'm strolling down the sidewalk, eager to get back to Donnie. The next, my brain clocks a familiar face—two familiar faces. My feet stumble to a stop and spin me around.

Half a block away, Miles and Wyatt are standing face-to-face, gazing into each other's eyes.

My heart is racing, but I take a few slow breaths and it calms down.

Wyatt wasn't lying then. They really are in love. It's

obvious even from this far away. I don't think Miles ever looked at me the way he's looking at Wyatt. Like he can't take his eyes off him. Like there's nothing else in the world that matters but him. It's hard to believe I never saw it when it was right in front of my face. Especially since I know what it looks like now—it's the way I look at Donnie.

I take another breath and I feel… annoyed more than anything else. I was having such a good day—I mean, all things considered—and I don't want Miles and Wyatt ruining it for me. I have less than zero interest in talking to them. Whatever affection or friendship I had there is gone now and I don't miss it. I'm fine. I'm good. I'm better than good.

"Connor?"

I jump and spin toward the voice, biting back a curse. Benedict and Zev are friends Miles and I used to go out on double dates with all the time. And from the way they're peering over my shoulder, faces painted with guilt, it seems like they're continuing the tradition—without me.

"How are you doing?" Zev asks. The concern lacing his voice makes my skin crawl.

As if he actually cares how I'm doing. Neither of them has reached out in the weeks since I walked in on Miles and Wyatt. All those times we sat at the same table, sipping mimosas over brunch, all those karaoke nights and getting drunk at a club—none of it meant anything to them.

Or if I'm honest with myself, to me. I haven't thought about brunch or karaoke or going out to a club. I haven't thought about Benedict or Zev or any of the people I used to call friends. They were never really my friends, were they? They always belonged more to Miles. Except for Wyatt and well… whatever, Miles can have him too.

"We're really sorry for what happened," Benedict adds when I don't answer right away.

I snort. Right, I don't believe that for a second.

"Where are you staying now? Are things okay?" Zev picks up.

I roll my eyes and hike my bags higher onto my shoulder.

"I'm fine," I say and strut off in the direction I came from. They can have their double date. I have something better waiting for me at home.

DONNIE

I end up sleeping *a lot*. Every time I open my eyes, Connor's there, either lying in bed next to me or set up in the armchair with his computer perched on his lap. He feeds me, keeps me hydrated, helps me shower, changes the bedsheets.

It's the second—or maybe third—morning when I finally wake up and don't feel utterly miserable. I stink. My clothes are soaked with sweat. But my body is oddly light when I sit up and my brain doesn't pound against the inside of my skull.

"Hey." Connor sets his laptop aside and comes to sit next to me on the bed. He puts his hand on my forehead. "You're not so hot anymore."

I give him a dead stare. "Gee, thanks."

He snorts and kisses the top of my head. "I meant your fever, silly. I think it broke."

I give my shoulders an experimental roll. There's only

lingering soreness, like I went for a long ride the day before. "Yeah, I think so too."

Connor holds out a new bottle of Gatorade. "Hydrate."

"Yes, sir."

He smirks as I down half the bottle.

"Thanks for taking care of me."

His cheeks glow a little pink. "You took care of me."

"Sounds like we take care of each other."

Connor's smile is soft. He gazes at me a little timidly and it's the most adorable thing I've ever seen. Warmth spreads through me that has nothing to do with the fever and everything to do with how much affection I have for him.

I hold my hand out and he comes to me, squeezing himself behind me so I can lean back against him. My eyes drift shut and I sigh.

I feel so much looser than I used to. I can breathe more easily and I swear my resting heart rate is lower now. It's a steady *thump-thump* that lulls me into an almost meditative state.

I let my thoughts drift to Roger and instead of the piercing pain I used to feel, there's a tender bittersweetness now. I'll always love Roger. I'll always miss him at least a little bit. But that suffocating weight of grief I've lived with for four years is gone.

That doesn't make what I have to do next any easier. "So, I was thinking..."

"Yeah?"

"I need to sort through Roger's things."

Connor kisses me on that spot where my jaw meets my ear. "I can help."

"Are you sure?" It doesn't seem all that fair to ask him

to help with this. It's something I should have done years ago. He shouldn't have to deal with the mess I've made for myself.

"Of course, if you want me to."

I snuggle back against him, a smile on my lips. How many guys would help his boyfriend clear out his dead husband's things? How many would sit there, listening to stories and asking questions about the dead husband? Not many. Connor is rare. He's a jewel.

"You know what else we need to do?"

"What's that?"

"Make an appointment to get tested."

The smile that grows on Connor's face shines brighter than the sun. "Okay, I will."

We eventually get out of bed. He offers to shower with me. I offer to cook us lunch—or is it dinner? I end up in the shower alone while Connor goes downstairs to the kitchen.

By the time I'm clean and feeling human again, Connor's got pasta boiling on the stove and ground turkey browning in the pan.

"I found the turkey in the freezer," Connor says, stirring the meat in the pan. "I hope it's okay I defrosted it."

"It's perfect." I hug him from behind and my eyes drift shut. It's so good just to hold him, to touch him, to have him in my arms. To think, I'd resigned myself to a life without this, without someone kind and compassionate and giving, without someone who makes me burn and fills me up.

His phone buzzes in his pocket and I slide my hand down his hip to fish it out for him. Connor looks at the screen and grumbles.

"Who is it?" I ask, not opening my eyes.

"Brad."

"What does he want?"

"To make sure I'm still going home for my parent's anniversary."

"You are, aren't you?"

"Yeah and I told him that. But he wants to double-triple check." Connor falls still in my arms. "He's asking if Miles is coming with me." His voice is strained.

I pull away from Connor so I can lean my hip against the counter and see his face. He's frowning at his phone and his shoulders are an inch higher than they were a second ago.

"I'm telling him now," he says quickly. His eyes flick to me, then back to his phone.

I didn't expect Connor to have told his family about me. I've only just told Phyllis and Leonard, after all. Our relationship is still delicately new, even if it feels like we know each other on a much deeper level already.

"Um, so…" Connor slides his phone back into his pocket. He takes the open jar of tomato sauce and pours it carefully on top of the turkey. "Would you… what do you think about… maybe, possibly coming with me? For the weekend?"

He's nervous and it's so endearing. He can't even meet my gaze. How can I say no to an invitation like that?

To be clear, the prospect of going through the whole "meet the parents" routine doesn't scream fun to me. I haven't gone through that since Phyllis and Leonard and that was almost two decades ago. A trickle of insecurity runs down my back. What will Connor's family think of me? I'm so much older than him. Widowed. We skipped over all the normal stages of dating and dove straight into living together.

What will happen if they don't like me? What will happen if I don't like them? I guess we'll find out.

"I would love to."

Connor's head snaps up. "Really?"

I chuckle at how wide his eyes are, like he can't quite believe his ears. "Did you think I was going to say no?"

"No, I mean, I don't know. Maybe?"

I drag him to me for a kiss, slow and sweet, punctuated with a tang of the tomato sauce he tasted straight from the pan. "If you want me there, I'll be there."

"I want you there."

Connor's food is simple, yet delicious. Or maybe that's just because I've had nothing but hot sodium water for the past couple days. Anything will taste better than canned soup. I still think it's good though, especially because of the chef.

After eating, I leave Connor in the kitchen to clean up while I go back to bed for a nap. I might not have a fever anymore, but even a couple hours of sitting around are enough to zap my energy. When I wake up, Connor's sitting in that armchair again, hunched over, neck extended, face illuminated by the light of his laptop. I grimace at the sight. My back twinges from watching him sit in that position.

"Doesn't your back hurt like that?"

Connor looks up and pulls his headphones down around his neck. He bends to one side, then the other. "Not really. Well, maybe a little?"

A sigh falls out of my lips. "Oh, to be young again."

He laughs and elbows the cushion behind him. "It's a comfortable chair!"

Yeah, I know it's a comfortable chair. I'm the one who bought it. But it's not meant to be used the way Connor's using it, and his back and neck and shoulders and everything are going to be angry with him in a couple years.

I push myself off the bed and grab my bathrobe from the foot of the bed. "Come on," I say, holding out my hand.

I lead him down to the second floor and the door that I've kept closed for the past four years. I put my hand on the knob, take a deep breath, then push it open. Roger's office looks exactly the way it did the last time I was in here. Unlike the last time though, I don't feel that crippling pain in the middle of my chest anymore. My lips curl into a smile and I step inside.

"This was Roger's." I run my hand along the giant desk he found at an antiques fair. It was almost too big to fit through the doorway. All his management books are still on the shelf. Our smiling faces are tacked to the corkboard on the wall.

There's a photo that was taken at a birthday party. I can't remember whose and I can't remember which year. We're young though, and we're happy. It doesn't hurt when I look at it, only that touch of bittersweetness.

I turn to Connor who's still hovering in the doorway. "Do you want it?"

Connor's brows draw together. "Want what?"

Look at him, so sweet. "The office, darling. It can be yours for when you're working from home. Or when you need a quiet space to write."

Connor's jaw drops to the floor. His gaze darts from

me to the desk to the chair to the bookshelf and back. "Are you serious?"

I can't take it. He's too cute. His eyes are so big. He can't seem to keep his mouth closed. He's like a kid who's been given free rein in the candy shop.

"Yes, of course I'm serious. Although, you'll have to help me clear out Roger's things, but then it's all yours."

I can imagine Connor here already, sitting at the desk, typing away on his computer. It'll be nice having someone use this room again. To have someone bring life back into what has become a mausoleum. But that's what Connor's been doing all along, hasn't he? He's lured me back from my doldrum existence and reminded me what it means to be me again. And now he's infusing some much-needed vibrancy into this old, empty house.

"You can switch up whatever you want. New chair. New desk. You should make the office your own."

Connor studies the desk for a bit, then pulls the chair out. He glances at me. "Can I?"

I nod and he sits down in it. The chair fits him. His posture is immediately better. When he pulls himself toward the desk, he takes on a confidence that I'm not sure he's experienced before. His shoulders are back, his chest is forward. He's sitting tall and smiling wide.

"What do you think?" he asks me, eyes bright and shining.

"It looks good on you," I say. It looks perfect on him.

"I think I'll keep this," he says, running his palms over the desk.

"It's yours," I say. All of it—all of me—is his.

CONNOR

I race up the subway stairs two at a time and almost trip over some dude's dog.

"Sorry!" I call out as I skirt around them.

Filming at the hotel in Midtown ran long. When I texted Donnie, he said he was saving me a bike, so I'd better be there. If I'm lucky, I'll make it just before the first song starts.

"Hey, Connor!" Sawyer nods to me as I rush into Mars.

I've already got my bag open and I'm digging through it, trying to find my gym pass.

"Don't worry about it." He waves me through. "You can scan it later."

"Thanks so much!" In the locker room, I change faster than Superman and I'm about to burst into the spin room when I skid to a stop at the door.

The class hasn't started yet. People aren't even on their bikes. More than a handful of guys are crowded around the sound system and even though I can't see past them, it's obvious that Donnie's the center of everyone's attention.

A tinge of jealousy runs up my spine and a sudden flash of insecurity has me rooted to the spot. He hasn't stopped being Donnie, The Spin Instructor, just because we're dating now. All these guys are still infatuated with him, hungry for his attention, willing to throw themselves at him.

"You should've called me! I would've nursed you back to health!"

Donnie's laughter rings out over their heads. "I already have my own personal nursemaid but thank you."

That eases some of my hesitancy and I inch forward.

"We're so happy you're back, Donnie." Whoever that is, he's laying it on so thick, it's almost lecherous.

"Seriously, Donnie. That sub was awful."

"He didn't push us hard enough."

"I didn't like the songs he used."

"I thought he pushed too hard."

Everyone's a freaking critic.

"Okay, all right." Two loud claps have the crowd scattering to their bikes. "Thanks, everyone. I'm glad to be back too, but we need to get the class started."

As the group thins, I finally catch sight of Donnie in his skin-tight cycling gear. The quick-dry material stretches across his muscular thighs and cups his dick in a mouth-watering bulge. The jersey molds to his flat stomach and the zip at the collar is open enough for me to catch a glimpse of his perma-hickey. The sight of it makes me stand a little taller, makes my chest puff up.

Donnie's eyes light up when they land on me and the smile he flashes is so intimate and familiar. It's something he saves just for me and I feel like the only person in the room. "Hey, you made it."

The room's silent now and I can feel the weight of a dozen stares on me. I don't care. I march up to him, take his hip in one hand and his cheek in the other, and kiss him. Hard, heavy, with enough tongue that there's no doubt about what's going on. Donnie's mine. He can have any of the gym bros at Mars but he chooses me.

Donnie makes a small sound when I pull away. His lips are rosy and his eyes are a little unfocused. The bulge in his bike shorts is noticeably bigger.

"Girl, that bitch? Are you kidding me?"

"Oh, Donnie. You can do so much better, honey."

"Damn, that's hot. Do it again!"

Heat shoots up the back of my neck and flashes across my cheeks. Christ, did I really kiss Donnie in front of his entire spin class? Yeah, apparently, I did.

Donnie smirks and nudges me toward a bike in the first row. "That one's yours."

It is? He usually saves me one in the back corner, where I like to hide. But there's something in the way he's looking at me now that makes me realize… we're not hiding anymore. His confidence seeps into me and I grab it with both hands.

"Let's get this party started!"

I hurry to the bike and climb on as the bass drops. Donnie's hunched over his bike handles and when I match his position, we can stare right into each other's eyes. I love this—the two of us focused on each other, riding together toward whatever future we want to make for ourselves.

"All right, everyone, let's find a nice and comfortable

pace. Not too hard, not too easy. This will be your baseline."

I fall into the rhythm of the class, pedaling in time to Donnie's legs, feeling the beat of the music booming through me. Donnie does that thing where he makes eye contact with everyone in the room, but his gaze always comes back to me. He always lingers for a few extra seconds.

It's the best class I've ever been to.

Fifty minutes later, I feel like I'm on top of the world. And sore enough that I'm about to fall right off of it.

"Great job, everyone!" Donnie shouts as he leads us racing past the finish line. He puts us through a cool-down routine, reminds us to hydrate, then dismisses the class.

I take my time wiping down my bike, keeping an eye on the sharks circling my guy. Donnie fends them off with practiced laughs. When the room is finally clear, he pulls me flush against his chest.

"Staking your claim?" His voice is a little husky and the sound reverberates straight to my balls.

"Maybe. A little."

"Hmm." He catches my lips in a sweaty, salty kiss that has me licking at him for more. He runs his hands down my back and gives me a hard slap on the ass. "Come on, let's go shower."

From the way he leers at me, I have a distinct feeling that we're going to get dirtier before we get cleaner. Donnie waits for me to grab my things from the members' locker room and then takes me into the staff one. It's a lot smaller, with only two rows of lockers with a bench running down the middle.

He takes my bag and dumps it into his locker, then

pushes me up against the metal doors and latches his mouth onto mine. "I don't want to wait until we get home."

My dick doesn't want to either.

He pushes us toward the showers as we tear at each other's clothes. He sticks his hands into the matching fish bowls next to the sink—one for condoms, the other for lube. We won't need condoms for much longer. Our appointment is scheduled for tomorrow and then a few days after that... The thought makes my dick leak in anticipation.

Donnie pulls me under the water, wrapping his hand around our dicks, squeezing them tight, and rubbing them together.

"Fuck, Donnie." My hips jerk and I thrust into his grip, the head of my dick catching on the rim of his. I shudder at the sensation and do it again.

"Did you see the death stares people were giving us?" Donnie murmurs into my ear. "They were so jealous. Of us. Of this."

Who can blame them? Me and Donnie? We're freaking fantastic together. I'm one lucky bastard. I get to touch him, kiss him, taste him. I know what it feels like to have his cock in my mouth, to have my dick in his ass, to hold him close while we breathe together.

"I wanna fuck you," I beg.

"Then fuck me." He rips open the pack of lube and squeezes half of it onto his fingers. He turns around and with one arm braced against the wall, he reaches behind himself with slick fingers.

I drop to my knees to watch. His ass muscles flex and relax, his hole opens up, and his fingers disappear inside.

My hands shake with need as I open the condom packet and roll it on.

I sink my teeth into the firm, fleshy part of his ass before standing and pulling his hand out of the way. Donnie's got both arms on the wall, back arched, ass stuck out for me. Water splashes across his body and he looks over his shoulder, eyes half-lidded, voice sultry. "What are you waiting for?"

Fucking hell, it's a miracle I don't come on the spot. "Just committing the view to memory."

I line myself up and we both groan as I sink into him. My body fits over his so perfectly, his back against my chest, my groin flush against his ass. I nip at his neck with my teeth and slide my hands all over his chest and stomach.

"Fuck, Connor. Give it to me, darling."

I love it when he calls me darling. It makes me feel so special, so precious. I pull back until only the head of my cock is inside him, then I snap my hips forward. Donnie's cry echoes off the tiled walls. Anyone in the locker room can hear him. Hell, people out on the main floor can probably hear him too.

Let them hear. Let them know what we're doing together, to each other.

I fuck him rough and dirty. We have time for slow and sweet later. His shoulders bunch and flex, his thighs shake from the force of my thrusts into his body. He takes every inch I have to offer. He sucks me in until it feels like my whole body is going to disappear inside him.

Donnie shifts his weight onto one arm and reaches down to grasp himself with the other. Then he's coming, clamping down on me like a vise, throwing his head back and biting his lip to keep his scream inside.

I ram myself as deep into him as I can go and join him, emptying myself out in him. I'll never get tired of this, of being inside him, getting all tangled up with him. I want to do it every day for the rest of my life.

Beau and Gavin are in the locker room when Donnie and I finally get around to cleaning ourselves up.

"Having fun?" Gavin asks, his eyes twinkling.

Donnie rolls his eyes and I try to duck behind him. "Yeah, we are," he says.

"It's a good thing we keep supplies handy then, isn't it?" Beau says dryly.

Donnie throws a glare in his direction and I get a sense the comment is part of a larger conversation. "Yeah, it is."

"Connor, Donnie tells us you're a filmmaker?" Gavin asks, as Donnie and I get dressed.

He keeps doing that, going around calling me a film-maker when I haven't made any films yet. "Uh, yeah, sorta."

"Not sorta. You *are*." Donnie says it like if he's emphatic enough, it'll make it true.

"Have you met Sebastian?" Gavin goes on.

The name doesn't sound familiar. "I don't think so."

"He's *sorta* a filmmaker too."

I don't know Gavin well enough to know if he's joking. "Oh yeah?"

"He makes porn," Beau says, like it's no big deal. Like every other person on the street makes porn.

My face goes hot. "Oh, uh, that's not the type of films I wanna make. I mean, not that there's anything wrong with that. Sex work is real work and all that. It's just… not… me…"

Donnie's smothering a laugh. Beau's shaking his head. Gavin comes over and slings an arm around my shoulder.

"That's cool. I just thought you two would have stuff to talk about. You know, like equipment and angles and stuff." There's enough innuendo in Gavin's voice that I wonder whether he's talking about equipment or *equipment*.

"Okay…"

"He's out front. Want to meet him?"

I shoot Donnie a questioning look.

"Go ahead. I've got a few things I need to finish up before I can go." He runs a towel through his damp hair one more time and then tosses it into the hamper.

"Awesome. We'll be out front." Gavin drags me out of the locker room and through the gym. "Sebastian's about your age. He's got his own production company and everything. It's pretty cool. We've let him use the gym as a set a few times."

He waves at a guy sitting at a table in front of the juice bar. "Hey, Sebastian!"

Sebastian looks up. He's cute. Dark hair and dark eyes. Super long lashes and a smile that somehow oozes sex and innocence at the same time.

"This is Connor. He's a filmmaker." Gavin pushes me into the seat across from Sebastian.

Sebastian lights up. "Oh, yeah?"

"Uh, yeah, but not like, um…" How do I say porn without saying porn?

"Porn?" Sebastian says it for me.

My face is red again and Gavin bursts out laughing.

"All right, kids. I'll leave you to it." He spins and marches away, leaving us to stare after him.

"Is he always like that?" I ask. I kinda feel like Dorothy, sucked up by tornado Gavin and spat out in another world.

"Overbearing problem-solver?" Sebastian chuckles. "Yeah, he is." He closes the laptop he's working on and leans forward. "So, tell me about your filmmaking."

He looks so earnest, so sincere, so I tell him about the screenplay I'm working on. About the gay couple inheriting this big, old haunted house. He listens carefully, almost like he's analyzing what I'm saying.

"What are your plans for production and distribution?" he asks when I finish.

My mouth hangs open, because otherwise, I'd laugh. Production and distribution? I'll be lucky if I can get the damn thing written. "I haven't thought that far ahead yet."

Sebastian nods and bends down for the bag at his feet. "That's cool. So, I sorta have my own production company."

"Gavin mentioned something about that."

He chuckles, shaking his head. "I figured. It's not a traditional setup though. More of a network of independent content creators. I help them produce high-quality films, facilitate collaboration, pool resources to get better reach."

He hands me a business card. It says Sebastian Silver and underneath it The Camboy Network.

"Anyway, I've been thinking about how to expand the network and I think you might be a good fit."

I snap my head up as butterflies explode in my stomach. "Really? But I don't make…" God, why can't I say the word? It's not like I've never watched any myself. I've watched plenty of it. Plen-ty.

"Porn?" Sebastian grins like this is something he's encountered before. "I know. I don't expect you to write naked dudes into your film. I mean, I won't object if you do. I love the idea of gay haunted house porn. But I like your idea too."

"So…" I need to make sure I understand what's happening here because it can't possibly be true. "You're offering to help me make my movie?"

"Yup."

"Why?"

Sebastian shrugs. "It sounds cool. I'm all about empowering people. Us little guys need to stick together."

I like it. It feels like an opportunity. It's not like anything I've ever seen before, but like Rick said, I have to know when to push on and when to back off. This feels like a push-on moment.

Donnie comes out from the back of the gym with one of the personal trainers I've seen around Mars. They're chatting as they approach our table, then the other guy bends down to give Sebastian a kiss.

Sebastian turns to me. "Have you met Christian?"

"No, nice to meet you."

Christian's a big guy with close-cropped hair and tattoos down both arms. Now that they're next to each other, I feel like I've seen them before somewhere.

"Ready to go?" Donnie asks, hiking both our bags over his shoulders. I take mine from him and give him a kiss in return.

"Yeah, I am." Ready to go anywhere with him.

DONNIE

"Darling, do you mind favoriting this song for me, please?" I sneak a quick glance toward Connor who's been staring out of the passenger window for the past twenty minutes.

He drags his gaze away and taps on my phone where it's clamped to the holder on the dash. "For your spin list?"

I'm always on the lookout for songs to design workout routines to and Connor has been kind enough to let us listen to a new music playlist while we drive up to his parents' anniversary weekend. "Yes, please."

Connor immediately goes back to staring out of the window and the sight of it makes my heart clench. He's been like this for days now. Sullen and sad, with the weight of the weekend settling heavier and heavier on his shoulders. I even suggested we put on a scary movie two nights ago and he opted to go to bed instead. That's when

I knew that the prospect of an entire weekend with his family is really bothering him.

I'm not exactly clear on what the problem is either. Connor can't seem to articulate it. He says they argue about nothing. They never apologize. Then they pretend it didn't happen and argue again. It goes around and around in a cycle that sounds exhausting. And frankly, unhealthy.

It's hard to know whether it's actually that bad. Connor has a tendency toward the dramatic, which I suppose fits with the whole storyteller and filmmaker thing. It does give me pause though, if they're really that nitpicky, how the hell are they going to react to me? I have to admit that this unknown factor has made me less than excited to spend an entire weekend in the same house as Connor's parents.

"I'm sure everything will work out."

Connor lets out a sigh filled with defeat. "I know. I'll be fine."

I hate that he feels this way, but short of turning around and going home, all I can do is be there for him. Perhaps his family will be less inclined to argue with a stranger in their midst.

It takes almost four hours to drive from Brooklyn all the way up to Springfield, Massachusetts. We get to the Hill's house with barely a minute to spare. Three generations of them are gathered out front and they all turn to stare when we pull up.

Connor slouches low in his seat. "Do I have to get out?"

"No, we can turn around and drive back to New York, if you want." I'm only half-joking. I wouldn't be opposed to turning tail and running.

"No, let's go. Brace yourself." Connor pops open the car door.

Well, that's not ominous at all.

An older version of Connor is standing in the driveway with his hands on his hips. "You're late." That must be Brad.

"You said dinner. I'm here before dinner."

Brad shakes his head and rolls his eyes. "At least you're here."

"Yeah, great to see you too."

Whoa, the tension isn't just palpable, it's thick enough to cut with a cold, dull butter knife.

A little girl breaks away from her mother and comes charging at Connor. His demeanor flips in an instant and he's smiling as he bends down to swoop her up and swing her around. "Hey, little girl!"

"I'm not little anymore!"

"Hey, big girl."

I catch Connor's wince as he sets her down and I bite back my smile. He's going to thank me for that proper office chair soon.

"Wait! I'm bigger than her!" Another girl has joined them now. The older sister, I believe.

Connor gives her a hug. "You're big too!"

"Come on, girls, go get in the car." Their mother comes to give Connor a kiss on the cheek. "Good to see you, Connor."

Then she turns an appraising eye to me. "I'm Hazel, Connor's sister-in-law."

"Lovely to meet you."

Her eyes light up when I shake her hand. It happens sometimes when I open my mouth—ah, the magic of the

British accent. She mouths a not-so-subtle "nice job" to Connor before turning back to corral her kids.

Connor's mother is right behind her, pulling him into a hug so tight, he's wheezing. "Hi, Mom," he squeaks.

She holds him at arm's length and pins him with a stare that even scares me. "It's about time."

"For what?" Connor sounds like a mouse.

"You've been away too long."

"I've been busy?" He doesn't sound certain.

Her eyebrow twitches and Connor flinches. "Too busy to visit your family?

Connor looks panicked for a moment before he turns to me. "This is Donnie!"

Great. Time to lay myself down on the sacrificial altar, it seems.

Except Connor's mother cuts a sideways glance at me before narrowing her eyes back on him. "Donnie with the fever?"

How did she know about the fever?

"Uh, yeah." Connor looks sheepish. There's something there that he hasn't told me about.

A polite mask drops over her face as she introduces herself. "Welcome, Donnie. I'm Kathleen. It's a pleasure to finally meet you."

I'm not sure what she's referring to but I can play along. "Likewise, Kathleen."

Brad comes up to physically lead her away. "Car. Restaurant. We're already late."

I don't think I'm going to like Brad.

An older man claps Connor on the back hard enough that I wince. Then he holds his hand out to me. He squeezes hard, so I squeeze back equally hard. Cycling isn't only about the legs, you know. The muscles around his eyes tighten just enough that I know he notices. "I'm Harold."

"Donnie."

"Enough chatting! Let's go! We can talk at the restaurant!" Yeah, I'm not going to like Brad, there's no question about it.

"We get it, we get it," Connor grumbles under his breath and I can't blame him.

I'm pulling the car away from the curb when I glance over at Connor. He's slumped in his seat again, arms crossed over his chest, staring out the window.

"How does your mother know I had a fever?"

His cheeks go pink and he drops his hand into his face. "I might've called her," he mumbles.

"What is that?" I ask because I can.

He glares at me. He knows I heard him the first time. "I called her, okay? You were passed out and I didn't know what to do."

Laughter bubbles up inside me, so bright and fizzy that I can't hold it in.

"Yeah, yeah, go ahead and laugh. It's not like you weren't dying or anything. Excuse me for worrying about you."

"Sorry! I'm sorry!" I reach for his hand and he lets me take it. "I'm not laughing at you, I swear. It's very sweet. You're adorable. Thank you."

Connor pouts and I want to tug him into my lap for a cuddle. He's usually so sunshine that when he gets grumpy, I can't help but tease. We drive the rest of the way like that, his hand in mine, and when I turn into the parking lot of the restaurant, I don't want to let go.

I shut off the engine and bring his hand to my lips. "Ready?"

Connor gazes at me through his lashes and my breath catches in my chest. He's so precious, my Connor. I want to give him everything. He leans toward me and I meet him across the middle console. He's been using my body wash and it smells good on him. He groans into my mouth and I scrape my fingers over his scalp, right behind his ear.

A knock reverberates from the passenger-side window and we both jump. Brad's bent over at the waist, peering in.

"Whenever you're ready to join us," he deadpans. He really is a jerk. No wonder Connor doesn't like him.

"I suppose we should go in."

Brad's made such a big deal about being late, but it only took us fifteen minutes to get to the restaurant, and it turns out that he booked the private dining room at the back. He's sitting at one end of the long table with Hazel and the kids. Kathleen and Harold are on one side of the table and Connor and I take the other.

Connor reaches under the table and I take his hand in mine. His shoulders drop an inch as we intertwine our fingers and my heart clenches a little more for him.

"So, Donnie." Kathleen looks back and forth between us. "How did the two of you meet?"

Connor has a vise grip on my hand and it might leave bruises. But he's got nothing to worry about because I've got it handled. "I'm a spin instructor at the gym where Connor's a member."

"You go to the gym?" Brad scoffs. "Since when?"

Oh, Brad had better watch himself or Connor's not the only one who's going to get goaded into a fight.

"I go to the gym," Connor shoots back.

"Boys," Kathleen says quietly but deadly, and they both snap their mouths shut. She smiles at me like she didn't just threaten the well-being of her only two children. This woman is fierce. "I've never done spin before. What's it like? It's the one with the bikes, right?"

I can answer this question in my sleep and I give her my most charming smile. I might lean into my accent too, but who's keeping track? "It is. The classes are fairly high-intensity. They're designed to be both cardio and strength training."

"I love spin!" Hazel chimes in from the other side of the table. "I mean, when I can get to a class. These two are my own private spin classes these days." I like Hazel. What is she doing with a guy like Brad?

One of the girls—Brooke, I think—tugs on her mother's sleeve. "Mommy, I can spin, too! Lemme show you." She tries to slide off her chair but Hazel very deftly keeps her in place.

"We know you can spin, honey. But not now. You can show Grandma and Grandpa some other time."

We're interrupted by waiters who bring dish after dish of Greek mezes until the entire table is overflowing. Brad's popping off descriptions of each plate as they come, like he's the one who made them. I have to hand it to him though, it's an impressive spread. Pastries and cheese and grilled meats and veggies. There's enough to feed all of us for a week. There's even a giant plate of fries for the girls.

"Donnie, am I correct in assuming that you're not from America?" Kathleen asks.

What gave it away? "You're correct. I'm from London,

but I've lived in New York for more than twenty years." No need to go into why I came, obviously.

"New York's expensive," Harold says to no one in particular. "Real estate prices are unreasonable. It's impossible for normal people to buy a house."

He's not wrong, though he sounds rather bitter about it. Maybe he wanted to get into the market but got priced out? He wouldn't be the first.

"Donnie owns his own place," Connor jumps in with pride in his voice.

I grit my teeth. That's not something I usually share right away. It tends to throw people off—how can a spin instructor afford an entire house in New York—and then I have to explain about inheriting the place and Roger's life insurance and all our savings. That's way more information than anyone needs to have. I can see it's having that effect around the table now.

"It's a brownstone. Three floors, plus a finished basement and a backyard." Connor sounds so pleased with himself and well, I can't hold it against him when he's beaming like that.

Harold doesn't look like he believes Connor though, and Kathleen's got a furrow between her brows. "That's… very impressive, Donnie. All that for yourself?"

Oh, no. Connor might have bragged us right into a corner. I glance over to see how he wants to play this. He looks guilty enough that there's no point in denying it. "Well, no, not anymore."

"I moved in." He fumbles for my hand under the table again and I give it to him.

Kathleen's staring daggers at him. "You moved in?"

Connor squirms in his seat. "Yeah, I did."

She opens her mouth, then clamps it shut into a tight-lipped smile. She cuts through a piece of roasted eggplant, her knife screeching across the plate.

I stab a piece of calamari with my fork and shove it into my mouth. Maybe if we're all too busy eating, we can forego any more conversation. The faster we get through this dinner, the better off we'll all be.

CONNOR

We climb back into Donnie's car and I slap a hand across my face. "Uggghhh." That was bad. Not the worst, but bad. "I'm sorry."

"What for?"

I gesture vaguely toward the restaurant.

"It was... okay." The words come out slowly like Donnie doesn't really want to say them.

I don't blame him. It was okay in the sense that no one raised their voice and no one got killed. But like, that's a really low bar.

I wish I'd taken him up on the offer to turn around and drive right back to New York. "Now do you understand why I don't like visiting?"

"Yes. Yes, I believe I understand perfectly now." He's still got his accent amped up and as much as I want to collapse into a heap of flesh and bones, there's one particular bone that perks up.

I reach into Donnie's lap and slide my palm up his thigh.

"Connor."

I love how he says it. *Con-ah*. With a touch of sternness that sends a shiver down my spine. His dick is a little chubby when I get my hand on it and it only takes a few gentle squeezes to get it nice and plump.

"Connor."

"Hmm?"

"I'm driving." And his knuckles are almost white as he grips the steering wheel.

Okay, no hand jobs—or blowjobs—while Donnie's driving the car. Although, when we get into a room with a bed… all bets are off. A couple orgasms are exactly what we need to let off some steam.

Mom's waiting for us when we trudge up to the front door with our bags. She has her hands clasped in front of her and she looks pointedly at me, then Donnie, before speaking. "I've made up the guest bedroom downstairs." She doesn't sound pleased—at all. "Connor, I'd like to speak to you once you've settled in."

My stomach sinks to the floor. I *do not* want to speak to my mother, not once I've settled in, not at any point tonight. I grab Donnie's hand and all but drag him to the staircase that leads down to the basement.

The guest room used to be our old playroom and when Brad and I moved out, Mom turned it into her craft room. There's a double bed in there, bins upon bins of yarn and fabric and shit, and Mom's sewing machine in the corner.

I flop onto the bed and Donnie sits down beside me. "Uggghhh." I fling an arm over my eyes.

"Everything's going to be fine. It's just for a couple of

nights." Donnie sounds like he's trying to reassure himself.

"I'm so sorry I dragged you into this." I honestly feel awful. Donnie shouldn't have to put up with all this drama.

He lies down next to me, head propped up on one hand. "I'm glad I came."

I cock an eyebrow at him, incredulous. "Really?"

"I think…" He trails his fingers up and down my stomach.

I suck it in when he gets a little too close to my ticklish zones. He ventures close, the tease, but never crosses the line.

"I might have thrown them off a bit."

"What do you mean?"

"I'm not what they expected."

Maybe. Donnie's certainly not like any of the other boys I've brought home. That's the whole point though, Donnie's not like anyone I've ever met. He's special. That's why I love him.

"I'm a lot older than you. I own a whole house." Donnie lifts an eyebrow. "They don't know about Roger, do they?"

I shake my head. "I haven't told them anything about that."

"Can you imagine what their reaction would be?"

I groan. I don't want to imagine it. "Let's not ever tell them."

Donnie chuckles and leans down to plant a kiss on the corner of my mouth. "They'll find out at some point."

"Yeah, but not now." I hook my ankle around his leg and pull him closer.

"Mmm, not now." His erection is thick against my thigh and I roll us so I've got him pinned underneath me. Donnie whimpers into my mouth.

"Connor?"

I jerk up. "Fuck."

Donnie muffles a giggle.

"Not funny."

"It's a little bit funny," Donnie whispers. "Your mother is cockblocking us."

"No fucking shit."

"Connor!"

"Yeah, I'm coming!" I push myself off Donnie and stare at my crotch. All it really takes is thinking about the conversation I'm about to have with Mom to make my dick shrink back into my body.

"Good luck," Donnie says.

"Thanks, I'll need it."

She's waiting for me at the kitchen table when I come up from the basement. Her fingers are wrapped around her nightly mug of tea.

"There's still some hot water if you'd like some." She nods to the kettle on the stove.

I hesitate. Will pouring myself a cup prolong this conversation? Or will it help distract me from it? I *could* use something to occupy my hands… I go pour myself a mug and sit down opposite her, watching the steam rise from my cup.

"So…" She has questions. She wants answers.

I don't know what or how much I want to tell her. "So…"

"What happened with Miles?"

Guess we're jumping right into it. "We broke up."

"I figured that much. Why? I thought things were going well."

I take a sip of tea and burn my tongue, then spend a good thirty seconds making a big deal of it. Mom doesn't look impressed but she doesn't rush me.

"Do we have to talk about it?" I know I sound like a petulant child. I *feel* like a petulant child.

Mom drops her gaze to her mug and she seems to deflate a little. "You know, there was a time when we talked about everything."

The words hit me deep in my gut. She's right. It was ages ago, when I was still a kid. I don't remember when that changed. Or how.

She lifts her gaze to me and I feel like I'm being assessed somehow, appraised to see if I measure up. Her lips twitch into something I think is supposed to be a smile.

"No, we don't have to talk about it if you don't want to." She stands and drifts to the sink.

This is *not* how I imagined this conversation would go. Where are the snarky comments and not-so-subtle jabs? Where are the disappointed looks and exaggerated eye rolls? It's like she's giving up and… no, that's not how this is supposed to work.

"He cheated on me," I blurt out. Oh, god. Why did I say that? I was *this close* to getting out of this thing Scott-free.

Mom frowns at me. "Miles did?"

"Yeah, with Wyatt."

Her eyebrows shoot up. "Why?"

"I don't know, Mom. Maybe because they're assholes."

Her lips press into a thin line. "There's no need to be calling names, Connor."

"If there's ever a time to be calling names, don't you think this is one of them?"

I can see the vein in her temple ticking and it drives away that slimy dismissive feeling I had. *This* is more like it. This is what we do. It twists my stomach into knots, but it's better than Mom turning her back on me.

"So out of the blue, Miles and Wyatt just start cheating on you." Her arms are crossed and she's leaning against the counter. She looks like she doesn't believe me.

"Yeah, Mom. I walked in on them."

"You *walked in* on them?" Her eyebrows are in her hairline now.

"Well, not like that." I throw my hands into the air. "I came home and Wyatt was scrambling to put on his clothes and Miles was coming out of the shower naked."

"There could be other explanations for that."

I shoot to my feet. Nope, I was wrong. I'd rather she turn her back. This argument is churning my insides so much I might hurl the dinner we ate all over the kitchen floor. "They admitted it to me, okay? They're in love with each other. I didn't *misunderstand* or *jump to conclusions*." Because that's exactly what she was going to say next, I just know it.

"How long ago was this?"

Why the fuck does it matter? "I don't know, a few months ago."

"And when did you move in with Donnie?"

I see where this is going. I drop back into the chair and pull my feet up onto the seat. It's too fast. It's too soon. You shouldn't jump into another relationship right away.

Donnie and I have been through all that. We've sorted it out. It's nobody's business but our own. "Not long after."

"Is that wise?" she asks, knowing full well that it's not a question. It's a judgment coached in a question so she can pretend she's not being judgmental.

"Yeah, it is," I say, because I know it's not the response she wants. "Donnie and I are good together. Like, really good. But I wouldn't expect you to know anything about that."

Mom flinches like I've slapped her across the face. Guilt floods into me, crashing against the anger and resentment until I don't know what the fuck I'm supposed to be feeling.

"What about the screenplay you're working on with Wyatt?"

I set my jaw. "We're not working together anymore."

Her frown deepens. "You're not going to try to reconcile?"

"Why would I want to do that?"

"Wyatt's your best friend."

"He *was* my best friend."

That's not sitting well with her and she turns on the faucet to wash her mug out. "So that's it? One incident and you're going to throw away the entire friendship."

I curl my fingers into fists. My nails dig into my palms and that little spark of pain is the only thing that keeps me from saying something I might regret. I *knew* she was going to be this way. So unreasonable and so unfair. Like this whole situation is *my* fault. Isn't she supposed to be on my side? She's my mother for fuck's sake.

She sets the clean mug on the drying rack and pats her hands on the towel hanging from the oven. When she steps back, her eyes are closed like she's trying to talk herself down from something. Disappointment wafts off her, so thick I almost choke on it.

"I'm sorry that this happened to you," she says. Her voice is quiet but her tone is edged with annoyance, like I'm forcing her to apologize or something.

It's the last straw. I can't be in the same room with her anymore. I rush out of the kitchen, not stopping when she calls my name.

I fly down the stairs, into the bedroom and slam the door behind me. I cringe at how loud it is. If Donnie wasn't here, Mom would probably come down here and tell me how disappointed she is about that too.

Donnie's already changed into his PJs, sitting in bed with his glasses on. His eReader is in his lap, forgotten, as he stares at me. Normally, I love the way Donnie looks when he's wearing his glasses. There's something so nerdy and intellectual about it that makes me hot.

But all I care about now is diving into the comfort I know I can find in him. From the concerned expression on his face, he probably heard every word Mom and I yelled at each other. He holds out his arms and I run into them. He's warm and solid and real. My rock when things go to shit. My anchor when things are slipping out of my control.

"Shh," he murmurs into my hair, hands running up and down my back. "I've got you. You're okay."

It's so much like that first night at Mars that I can't stop the tears from leaking out of my eyes. I bury my face into his chest. I don't want to cry. I have no reason to. Fighting with Mom is not a new thing—I was expecting it all along. It's just...

God, I don't even know. I hate the fighting but I hated that moment when it felt like she'd given up on me even more. Why are those the only two options? Why can't she be supportive like Donnie is?

I'm wrung out. Hollow. My head is throbbing.

Donnie shifts, trying to roll me onto my side. I lock my arms and legs around him. "I don't need to fucking hydrate," I mutter.

He chuckles and presses a kiss to my temple. "Okay, no hydrating. Let's just get you out of your clothes."

I let him move me like I'm a rag doll, stripping off my clothes and pulling on my PJs. He tucks us in, my head on his shoulder, my arm around his waist, my leg thrown over his thighs. This is where I'm meant to be.

I snuggle into him, breathing his woodsy, citrusy scent. I can feel the steady rhythm of his heartbeat and the slow rise and fall of his breathing. I sigh. "I love you."

DONNIE

It takes me a long time to fall asleep.

I love you.

Connor's softly murmured words echo through my head, through my heart. He was barely conscious when he said them, already overwrought from the argument with his mother. He might not have meant it. He most likely didn't even realize he'd said it.

I manage to sleep for a few hours only to wake again at first light. The first thought that rocks through me is Connor's *I love you* and it makes my heart ricochet around in my chest. Fear creeps up my spine and trepidation roils in my stomach. Does he really mean it? What if he does? What if he doesn't?

I shouldn't read too much into it. I shouldn't draw any conclusions until we've had a chance to talk about it like adults. The problem is, I don't know which answer I want to hear.

I ease myself out from under Connor's heavy body and

sneak out to the bathroom across the hall. Splashing some icy water on my face doesn't help with the nervousness gripping me. I need to move, I need to ride, I need to do something that will work off the excess adrenaline in my system.

Connor's still out cold when I quietly let myself back into our room to change into my running gear. I'm not a runner—it's too hard on my knees—but it's better than nothing when I don't have any other options.

I make sure I have my phone and earbuds with me and leave the house through the sliding glass door in the kitchen. The gate between the backyard and the front yard is unlocked and I make sure it's latched before I take off.

I have a running-specific music playlist with exactly the right beats per minute to help regulate my pace. This neighborhood is peak suburb, where all the houses are two-storied and detached with long driveways and perfectly manicured lawns. The streets bend and curve, some end in cul-de-sacs, and random little parks pop up when I least expect them to.

I run, losing myself in the steady left-right, left-right, letting the music drown out all the what-ifs packed into my brain. My smart watch buzzes at the one-mile marker. Then at the two. I'm just shy of three miles when I roll to a stop in front of the Hill house again to cool down and stretch.

My head is clearer now. My heart rate is elevated but I can tell it'll settle into something nice and low once I've cooled down completely. I still don't know what I'm going to do about Connor's unconscious revelation though.

Kathleen is in the kitchen when I let myself back in.

She's standing by the sink, cradling a mug of what I really hope is coffee, her expression inscrutable.

"Good morning," I greet her, bracing myself for her reaction.

"Good morning," she responds softly, like she's still in the process of waking up. She nods toward the coffee machine on the counter. "There's coffee if you'd like. Help yourself."

I would like, so I do help myself. "Thank you for having me here this week," I say, because it's the polite thing to do and because Kathleen doesn't seem inclined to fill the silence.

She chuckles ruefully. "You're welcome. Although, I can't imagine it's been very pleasant for you."

Whatever does she mean? I doubt she'll appreciate my snark though, so I keep it to myself.

"We weren't always like this, you know—the bickering." She's staring out of the window now, almost as if she's talking to herself. "It only started after Connor moved away for school. It was like we forgot how to talk to each other all of a sudden. It gets worse every time he comes home and now he barely comes home at all."

Sadness is radiating off her, thick and heavy, and it's getting me all choked up. It's obvious to me that she loves her son very much. She just expresses it in kind of an odd way. It's a shame really, to see this chasm between Connor and his mother that they both hate. It's like they're running toward each other so hard that they can't—or don't know how to—stop before they crash.

"He doesn't like the arguing either," I say, just in case Kathleen believes otherwise.

She shoots me a skeptical look.

"It's true. It's why he doesn't visit very often, to avoid the arguing."

Kathleen's expression falls. "I know. I tell myself every time that it's going to be different this time. We're not going to fight. We're going to get along. And then…" She shakes her head. "Something always happens. I'll say something wrong. Or he'll say something that sets me off."

"What was it last night?" It's none of my business and she has every right to tell me so, but I want to know. I want to fix this for Connor. I want to help him mend his relationship with his mother, if I can. He wants to and she wants to. Maybe all they need is a little perspective, someone from the outside who can point out things they can't see for themselves.

"I don't know." Kathleen lets out a dry laugh that's more painful than happy. "I asked about Miles and he told me about the affair. Then I asked about Wyatt and whether they were going to reconcile. And then…" She throws her hand up in a helpless gesture.

I think I see where the problem is. "He beat himself up for a long time about whether he should keep working with Wyatt."

Her scowl doesn't budge but she does take a moment to process the new information. "He can be so impulsive sometimes."

That's news to me. I haven't seen Connor make any decisions without going back and forth at least a dozen times.

"He does things that don't make sense to me. I don't know how to help him and when I try to help, I always seem to get it wrong. And I'm sorry, you don't need to have your boyfriend's mother offloading on you like this."

She sets her mug down and starts moving about the kitchen, pulling things from cabinets and drawers.

"I don't mind," I say over the clanging of bowls and plates and utensils.

Kathleen stops, one hand on the edge of the counter, the other on her hip, as she breathes through whatever is going on in her head.

"You know," I say carefully. I'm venturing into dangerous territory here and the last thing I want is to make things worse between Connor and Kathleen. "I'm not sure he needs you to help in the way you're trying to help."

She cuts a glare at me and yeah, I need to tread lightly.

"I think he just needs you to be there for him. And if he wants help, he'll ask for it."

She doesn't believe me. I scramble.

"It's like when I was sick. He called you to ask what he should do, right?"

Kathleen straightens and crosses her arms. Her glare is replaced by something more contemplative that says, "go on."

"You were the first person he went to. Because he knew you'd be there for him and that you'd know what to do."

She tilts her chin up. "I've never thought about it that way before."

"It's not that he doesn't want your help. He just doesn't need it as much as you might think he does. You've raised a really smart and capable son, Kathleen. I think he's learned more from you than you realize."

Her expression softens and she sniffles. She turns back to the carton of eggs she pulled out of the fridge and starts cracking them into a shallow bowl. Have I been dismissed? Does she want me to stick around? Is she making French toast for breakfast?

"You know," she says, not bothering to turn away from her cooking. "I'm glad Connor has someone like you in his life. I think you'll be good for him."

Relief washes through me and I let out the breath I hadn't known I was holding.

"His past boyfriends have been… meh." She shrugs, unimpressed. She pauses, whisk in hand, and studies me. "But you're different."

I want to be different. I want to give Connor things he's never had before, things he can't get anywhere else. I want to be as good for him as he's been for me—and that's a tall order.

Affection wells up inside of me, filling up every abandoned pit and every forgotten corner. It grows and grows until it feels like I'm overflowing with it, like I'm going to drown in it. No, it's not merely affection, it's so much more than that. It's deeper, stronger, more potent. If it's not quite love yet, then it's well on its way there. It's only a matter of time.

"I'll do my best to take care of him," I say to Kathleen, the emotion making my voice crack.

She smiles, a little sad and resigned, but more than anything else, hopeful. "Thank you."

CONNOR

I'm sitting at the top of the stairs, getting all teary-eyed and choked up. When Donnie lays it all out like that, I feel like such an ungrateful child. And also, entirely vindicated at the same time. He makes it sound so simple, so obvious, while Mom and I have been ruthlessly going at each other's throats.

I need to cut Mom some slack, I think. I should let her in a little more, let her help a little more. I can't keep coming to every encounter with my shields up and defenses primed. Not if I want our relationship to improve. And I do.

"Hey."

I squawk and almost fall down the stairs. I've got one hand on the banister and the other on the step, heart somewhere up in the attic of the house. Donnie's standing above me, holding two mugs and smirking.

"What are you doing?"

I right myself, comb my fingers through my hair, and

tug my shirt straight. I clear my throat, still groggy from sleep. "Nothing."

"Nothing? You weren't eavesdropping?"

I drop my jaw and flop a hand over my chest. "I would never!"

"Hmm." Donnie narrows his eyes. "I was on my way down to bring you coffee."

I make gimme hands at him. "And I was meeting you halfway." I take the mug he offers and hold it to my nose. Ah, the sweet scent of caffeine-laced sugar and milk. I take a sip and gaze over the rim of the cup at Donnie.

My breath catches in my chest at the way he's watching me, like he's studying every eyelash, the angle of my nose, the curve of my brow. Like he's trying to soak in every inch of me because he can't get enough. Like I'm the only thing he ever wants to look at for the rest of his life.

"Come here," he says and I take the two steps up to meet him.

He pulls me into a kiss. Our lips fit together like they were made for each other. He tastes like bitter coffee but underneath it is the sweet familiarity of Donnie. Woodsy and citrusy and I want to crawl inside him and live there.

His tongue delves into my mouth, slow and sensual, deep and so fucking erotic. He kisses me like I'm oxygen, like I'm water, and he needs this kiss to live to the next minute. He kisses me like I'm his everything.

I'm coming apart at the seams from this kiss, falling to pieces as his tongue slips into every corner of my mouth and licks over every inch. I cling to Donnie, my knees weak, and my limbs liquid. My cock is harder that fucking steel.

"Ahem."

Someone clears their throat behind me and I jump, spilling hot coffee all over my hand.

"Fuck!" I stick the burned spot into my mouth and glare at Dad who's standing there with his hands in his pockets, like it's a normal occurrence for him to stumble upon his son making out with his boyfriend at the top of the staircase. I flush so hot, my cheeks burn. "Jesus, Dad. Way to sneak up on us."

"Well, it is my house."

"Sorry about that, Harold." Donnie pulls me to the side so Dad can get into the kitchen. He smirks at me once Dad is out of the way.

"Ugh, god," I groan.

Donnie gives me a peck on my cheek. "I need to go shower. I believe your mother is making French toast."

Ooo, my favorite. "Hurry. Can't promise there'll be any left if you take too long."

Donnie disappears down the stairs and I take a deep breath before joining my parents. Dad's already sitting at his spot at the table, coffee in hand, with the news pulled up on his tablet. Mom drops a piece of egg-drenched toast into the pan and the sizzle makes my stomach growl.

They look so normal. Like the dinner wasn't the most awkward thing ever last night. Like I didn't have an argument with Mom afterward. Like she didn't have the deepest heart-to-heart with my boyfriend this morning.

"Hey," I say, wiping down my dripping mug and refilling it.

"Good morning, dear," Mom says. "Do you mind setting the table, please? Your brother's coming over for breakfast."

Great. Love it when Brad shows up first thing in the morning.

Donnie's quick in the shower and he makes it to the table as Mom piles on a full breakfast of eggs and bacon and sausage and French toast.

"This smells fantastic, Kathleen. Thank you so much."

Mom beams and shoves an extra piece of sausage onto Donnie's plate. His smile is polite, but I see the way it tightens on one side.

I lean over to whisper in his ear. "Would you rather your protein pancakes?"

Donnie shoots me a look that says "behave." I shoot back another that says "make me."

"So, Mom, Dad, you'll be taking off soon, right?" Brad asks, stuffing his face with bacon.

"I don't know why we can't stay to help." Mom's already at the sink washing up before she's even sat down to eat a bite.

"Because it's your anniversary party. You can't do any of the work."

"I don't see why not," she mutters.

Brad ignores her. "Just go play your golf. Make sure you're back here by one o'clock."

"You don't need us to help with anything, do you?" I pour an extra dollop of maple syrup on my toast, knowing Donnie isn't going to let me anywhere near the stuff when we get home.

"No." Brad doesn't even look in my direction. "The party supplies people and the caterer will be here soon. They're bringing their own staff."

Good, because I have no intention of staying here and

letting him boss me around. I grab Donnie the second breakfast is done and we're out the door before Brad can change his mind.

"Where to?" Donnie asks as we buckle ourselves into the car.

"Um… there's Forest Park?" I pull the directions up on Donnie's phone and we head toward the large park kinda in the middle of the city. It's busy when we get there. The baseball diamonds are filled with kids in uniforms, their parents yelling from the sidelines. People are out jogging or walking their dogs or having picnics on the grass. Fluffy white clouds dot the sky and the sun is warm on our skin. I take Donnie's hand in mine and we meander our way through the park.

"Tell me about growing up here," Donnie says as we step off the path to let a couple joggers pass.

I think back to high school, to my childhood, and not much stands out. Typical suburban upbringing in a typical suburban family. "It was pretty boring, to be honest."

Donnie eyes me with an amused look. "I find that difficult to believe."

"It's true!" I laugh, feeling almost giddy with happiness. Just being here, in the beautiful weather, with Donnie, it's inconceivable that life can be anything other than perfect. "My parents couldn't drag me away from the TV. I was in the AV club in high school. Did the sound for all our musical productions. Filmed them too."

"You really are a film geek." Donnie nudges me with his shoulder and I giggle—yep, full-on giggle.

"I had an early start."

"Who was your first kiss?" he asks.

I groan. "Isaac Paulson in freshman year. At the back of the auditorium during rehearsals."

"Ooo… in a dark theater. How dramatic."

"Yeah, yeah. How about you?" I nudge him back with my shoulder.

"Susan McDonald at the neighborhood football pitch," Donnie answers wistfully.

I gasp. "A girl!"

Donnie laughs and tries to shush me at the same time. "Don't go ruining my gay cred now."

He's joking, I know, but I still glance around and spot a few people staring at us. They all avert their eyes when they realize I've caught them. One teenager flashes me a tiny smile before he turns back to his friends.

"When did you come out?" Donnie asks as we take the right fork and venture into a less populated area of the park.

"Summer before high school. My parents had already guessed, so…" I shrug. "I told my mom and she was like, 'Cool, no boys allowed in your room.' That was it."

"Anticlimactic. It's better that way."

I suppose he's right. Fourteen-year-old Connor had wanted more of a reaction. Not anything like what happened to Donnie of course. But a few stray tears wouldn't have hurt either.

Looking back, homophobia had never really been a real fear for me. My parents didn't make a big deal out of it. My school had a no-bullying policy that they were good about enforcing. I wasn't the only queer kid in my class either. I'd never had to think about pretending to be someone I wasn't, or worry about how other people were going to react when they found out.

I know Donnie's story is exactly the opposite and a fit of righteous anger burns in me toward his parents. "Can you tell me how you came out? Only if you want to."

Donnie's hand tightens on mine and I drift a little bit closer to him as we walk. "I'd just finished uni. There'd been a big public health campaign for gay men to get tested for HIV. The ads were all over the city—you couldn't miss them. I'd gotten tested with some friends but then my dad found the results in my room."

My chest is tight, bracing for what's coming next.

"I guess I could have said that straight men get HIV too, but there wasn't any point. They wouldn't have believed me. I never talked about girls, never brought a girl home to meet them. It was pretty obvious."

I press a kiss to his shoulder and hug his arm to me.

"They told me to get out. I stayed with a mate for about six months. Got a job at a bank, got transferred to America, then I met Roger." He smiles, nostalgic and a little melancholy. There isn't the same weight or dreariness that he used to have when he spoke about Roger or his family. There hasn't been since he visited Roger at the cemetery.

"And well, you know the rest."

"You haven't spoken to your family since then?

Donnie shrugs. "I have a few times. I sent them Christmas cards and birthday cards at first. But I never got any back. I called them when Roger and I were getting married. They were civil but they weren't happy about it. They didn't come to the wedding and I kind of gave up after that."

Donnie's conversation with Mom this morning echoes through my mind. We might have a dysfunctional relationship, but at least we still have a relationship. I can't imagine never speaking with her again. No more annoying texts from Brad? No more rambling lectures about things I don't care about from Dad? I feel a little panicked at the mere possibility.

"Roger and I made our own family. Phyllis and Leonard were wonderful to me and we had a lot of friends. We were always hosting parties at the house for birthdays, when someone got promoted or started dating someone new. Basically, any excuse we could find to throw a party." Donnie's smile fades. "I haven't been very good at keeping in touch with them."

There are a lot of people in all those photos Donnie has around the house. But other than the guys from Mars, I've never heard him talk about other friends. "Why not?"

He gives a half-hearted shrug. "It was hard at first. Everyone was tiptoeing around me all the time, asking if I was okay, if there was anything they could do. I know they meant well, but... I wasn't okay, there wasn't anything they could do, and I got so tired of them asking. I stopped going out when they invited me and eventually, they stopped inviting me."

My heart aches for Donnie. I wish I'd known him back then, that I could've been there to help him through it. I would've just held him, let him cry, let him rage, whatever he needed to do.

"And now? Would you want to reconnect with them?"

Donnie drops his gaze to the asphalt under our feet. "I should."

"But?"

He shakes his head. "But nothing. I have no excuse other than... it's a little awkward, that's all."

An idea pops into my head. I think I saw Donnie's

birth date marked on one of the cards in Roger's office. It's soon—in a few weeks. Any excuse to throw a party, right? If this isn't the perfect way to help Donnie get in touch with his old friends again, I don't know what is.

CONNOR

At twenty to one o'clock, Donnie drags us back to the car so we're not late for the party. I don't want to leave the park. I'd rather spend the afternoon with him, doing literally anything but go to the party. I'd even go to like, a nutritional diet seminar with him if he wanted.

But nope, Donnie's all about doing the right thing, so we drive back to my parents' house, only to find we can't actually drive *to* the house. There are cars lining the curb down the entire block and around to the next one too. We finally find an empty spot two streets away and walk back.

How many people did Brad invite? The answer is a lot. But then, my parents know a lot of people. It's not just all of our extended family—aunts and uncles and more cousins than I can count. It's also all their friends from decades in the workforce and bowling leagues and knitting clubs and oh my god, the backyard is a zoo. There's gotta be a fire code violation in here somewhere.

We're no more than two feet inside the backyard when I'm ambushed and I lose my hold of Donnie's hand.

"Connor! Where've you been?" Alisha, my cousin, crushes me in a hug.

"Yo, dude. You come back and you don't even let us know?" Nate, her brother, gives me a crushing hug too.

"Hey, Mr. Big City! When'd you get here? How long are you staying?" Candace, yet another cousin, is next in line.

"I just got here yesterday and I'm leaving tomorrow and surprise! I'm here!" I look around for Donnie but he's disappeared into the crowd.

"Have you lost weight?" Alisha asks, pushing me away so she can give me a once-over.

"Nice thighs. You're not skipping leg day, are you?" Nate jokes.

"Uh, something like that." I haven't lost weight. In fact, I might weigh more from all the spin classes and healthy eating that Donnie's got me doing. Speaking of, where is he? I crane my neck to see over the tops of people's heads but there's no signature salt and pepper hair in sight.

"What's up? You looking for someone?" Candace asks.

"Sorta. Um, have you seen an older guy? Kinda silver fox-y?"

"Silver fox, huh?" Alisha turns to help me look. "That guy?"

I follow her pointed finger and yep, there's Donnie with what I suspect is cranberry juice and soda water, talking to someone I don't recognize.

"Yeah, thanks." I squeeze between Nate and Candace, ignoring their protests about abandoning them. I can't abandon them when they trail after me in a single file like lemmings.

The woman Donnie's talking to excuses herself right before I get there.

"Who was that?"

"A friend of your mom's. They do some sort of crafting thing together." Donnie's eyeing the posse of cousins who've followed me across the backyard. "Hi…"

Nate jumps in before I can introduce them. "Hey, I'm Nate. We're Connor and Brad's cousins."

"I'm Candace."

"Alisha. And you are?"

"This is Donnie," I say, trying to wrangle back control of the situation. "He's my boyfriend."

All three sets of eyes snap to me. "Boyfriend?"

"What happened to that other dude? What's his name?"

"Miles. What happened with Miles?"

"I mean, I'm sure you're great, Donnie. Do you work out?" Alisha's feeling up Donnie's bicep and he takes a sip of his cranberry soda, using the cup to hide his smirk.

"Yes, he does work out. Donnie's a spin instructor. And Miles is no longer in the picture, so can we just let that go?"

Alisha and Candace exchange a look and I know I'm not going to escape their interrogation later.

Nate's stepped in front of everyone, like we're all invisible, to talk to Donnie. "Spin instructor, huh? You know anything about intermittent fasting? Does that help build muscle?"

It's like that for most of the party. The five of us staked

out around a table in the corner of the backyard, taking turns grabbing food and drinks from the buffet table and bar. Donnie fits right in with my cousins and answers way too many questions from Nate. I catch up with Alisha and Candace, about the guy Candace is seeing and the horrible dates Alisha's been on recently.

At one point, Brooke and Aurora come rushing up to us. They finally get to put on that spinning demonstration their mother thwarted, and end up flat on the ground giggling their heads off. Donnie, as the resident spin professional, declares them expert spinners.

The sun dips below the horizon and lanterns flicker to life all around the backyard. Brad's had fairy lights strung up overhead and they look like stars blinking against the night sky.

I drape an arm around Donnie's shoulders and he leans into me like we've been doing this for years. This is really nice. I'm really happy. It floors me.

I thought I was happy back in that apartment with Miles, working at random coffee shops with Wyatt. Now I know that was a poor facsimile of happy—not even that, it's like the third layer down on one of those old carbon copy things, the writing so faint you can't read it anymore. I might have gone through life thinking that's all there was to it if I hadn't walked in on Miles and Wyatt that day.

My life is so much more now. A beautiful house with my own freaking office and a legit-ass theater room. I've got an exciting new screenplay and someone who wants to help me develop it into an actual film. But most importantly, I've got a sexy, sophisticated, caring man who I get to go to sleep with every night. This is real happiness. I wouldn't trade it for anything.

The music dies down and the sound of clinking glass draws everyone's attention to the raised deck where Brad is standing with Mom and Dad. He's holding a glass of champagne.

"Thank you, everyone, for coming to Kathleen and Harold's fortieth-anniversary party. I'd like to make a toast, so if you need a drink refill, now's the time to get it."

"Anyone?" Alisha asks the table before slipping out of her seat to go to the bar.

"Mom, Dad, forty years. Damn, that's a long freaking time."

Chuckles ripple out through the crowd.

"You know, when you're a kid, getting married, or becoming a parent, they're just things you do one day. You don't question it, whether it's something you even want or how difficult it might be. At least, I never questioned it. It was always a given for me.

"And I know, some of you might think that I was going through the motions of life or whatever. But I think the reason I never questioned it was because of you, Mom and Dad. I mean, it's not like you never fought or you were always the perfect parents—"

"Hey, watch your mouth, young man," Dad interrupts to a spike of laughter.

Brad waves his hand to calm the crowd. "What I was going to say was that you made it look easy, you made it look fun, like that was the best possible thing I could do with my life. Why the heck would I want to do anything else."

I snort, because like, what the fuck. There's an entire world of other things people might want to do. *Not everyone wants the white picket fence, the giant SUV, and two-*

point-five kids, Brad. No offense to Brooke and Aurora. Donnie pinches my side where he knows I'm ticklish. "Hey, no fair."

On the deck, Mom's sniffling, blinking tears from her eyes and yeah, I guess it's a good toast and all, but seriously?

"And then I actually got married and I actually had kids and well..." Brad grimaces. "Either you two have some secret sauce you're not sharing or you're really good fakers."

"They're really good fakers!" someone in the crowd shouts.

"Right? Because marriage is hard and being a parent is hard and oh my god, I'm so tired all the time. Were you tired all the time?"

Mom and Dad both nod. "All the time," Mom says.

"Forty years and you haven't killed me or Connor. You haven't killed each other. That's a huge accomplishment in my books." Brad finds his wife a few feet away. "I only hope that Hazel and I can do as well as you have."

He raises his glass. "So, here's to Kathleen and Harold and the next forty years. Happy anniversary!"

The party ripples with more well wishes and I drain the rest of my beer. There's nothing wrong with Brad's little speech. There's nothing wrong with celebrating forty years of marriage—I get it, it's impressive. Except it feels like we're painting right over all the ways that this family *doesn't* work.

The conversation between Donnie and Mom notwithstanding, she and I haven't actually said anything to each other that sounds remotely like we're trying to change. I want to change. I hope we do. I'm just not super optimistic when it comes to my family.

Donnie squeezes my knee. "Hey, you okay?"

"Yeah, I'm fine."

He doesn't believe me and that's fine too. My gripes aren't something that can be fixed in a day, with a single conversation. The important thing is that Donnie's here.

It's another hour or so as the party winds down. We say goodbye to Alisa, Nate, and Candace, then escape downstairs and lock the door behind us.

I push Donnie up against the door and my fingers get to work on the buttons of his shirt.

Donnie chuckles. "Everyone's still upstairs, darling."

"So?" I nip at his collarbone as I push the two sides of his shirt apart. "We'll be quiet." I find the spot on his neck where his pulse beats steady and strong. There's no hickey there at the moment—in deference to my parents—but I swirl my tongue in circles, wishing I could seal my lips onto his skin. Soon. Tomorrow. The perma-hickey is going back in place.

Donnie slants his mouth across mine, licking his tongue into me the way he did this morning. There's so much intention in the kiss, so much deliberate worship that my knees go weak and I pin Donnie to the door.

He pushes me away and I tumble onto the bed. Donnie doesn't follow me right away. He detours to his bag where he pulls out a travel-sized bottle of lube, then steps out of his pants. I strip off my clothes and scoot back to lay my head on a pillow. Donnie climbs up over me, straddling my hips, his cock already hard and jutting out from his body.

He's like a fucking god, looming over me like that, every muscle standing out in sharp relief. Thighs so thick, they could flatten me into a pancake. That ridiculously cut V that acts like a runway leading down to his dick.

I reach for him. I need to feel his skin under my palms. I need to squeeze his muscles and have them move under my touch. Donnie puts his hands over mine, guiding me where he wants me to go. His nipples, his sides, that crease where his ass meets the backs of his thighs. I cover every inch of his body that I can reach before he takes my hands and pins them above my head.

My entire body shudders at what's coming next. Donnie's grin is devious. He's going to take me apart and we both know it. He doesn't just bend his head down to lick my armpits. He lowers his whole body to slither along mine. His cock is hot on my stomach and I jolt in pleasure when it rubs against mine. His chest is this hard expanse that I arch into. When his tongue makes contact with my armpit, my cock jumps and I let out a deep, guttural groan.

"Shh," he whispers in my ear. "We wouldn't want everyone to hear us."

It's unlikely they will. The people Brad hired are stomping in and out of the backyard as they tear down the party. They're generating more than enough noise to drown us out. Still, I swallow down my groans as Donnie resumes his delicate torture.

I can't keep my hips on the bed. My dick needs to be inside Donnie. It needs the hot vise of his ass so much it fucking hurts. "Donnie, please, I can't take it anymore."

I don't actually expect him to listen to me—he usually never does. But this time, he presses the lube into my hand

and straightens so he's kneeling above me again.

"Get me ready then."

The bottle slips out of my hand twice as I try to open it and squeeze the slippery lube out. Donnie chuckles and smirks but doesn't try to help me, the bastard. His eyes drift shut when I reach behind his balls though, running my fingers across his taint and back toward the sacred entrance to his body.

Donnie holds himself open for me and the sight is breathtaking. His lithe, long body. Gorgeous cock, hard and standing at attention. His arms flexed as he's pulling his ass cheeks apart, all so I can push my fingers inside.

I take my time, circling the wrinkled skin, then slowly pressing in. I slide in easily. Donnie's well-versed in letting me in by now. He relaxes into the invasion and makes these little mewling sounds at the back of his throat that trip something primal and possessive in me.

Donnie's mine. I love him and he's mine. Other guys can look, sure, but they'll only be reminded of what they're missing out on.

I'm trying to work in a third finger when Donnie stops me. He slicks up my cock where it's straining to get inside him, then lines us up.

Holy Jesus Christ. We got our test results back as we were leaving for Springfield. Two completely clean bills of health. I know Donnie packed condoms along with the lube, but I guess we're not using those anymore. The head of my dick nudges against Donnie's entrance and it already feels as hot as hell.

"Connor."

I drag my eyes away from that spot between Donnie's legs and when I look up at him, our gazes collide. It's staggering. The way Donnie's looking at me. There's lust and want and desire. Then there's more—affection, tenderness, and… I don't want to think it, just in case it's not true. I want it to be true so damn badly, I want Donnie to love me so much that if he doesn't, it might destroy me.

Donnie locks our eyes together as he sinks down on me. My jaw drops open in a silent scream as I'm engulfed in the hottest, tightest, most mind-shattering grip I've ever had the honor of feeling.

I don't breathe until he's fully seated on me. And when he starts moving, starts fucking himself on me, I know I'm not going to last long. "Donnie," I say, still staring into those beautiful hazel eyes.

"I know, darling. I know." His hand is working his cock as he shows off how strong his thighs are. His ass is milking me for everything I'm worth.

It's so good and I'm so close. I hold Donnie by the hips and plant my feet flat on the mattress. I slam my hips up into him as I pull him down on me.

Donnie's eyes go wild. "Fuck," he grinds out.

I do it again. And on the third time, Donnie's coming all over my stomach, spurt after spurt of creamy white cum that feels like molten lava on my skin. I let myself go, pumping myself again and again into Donnie's body, as deep as I can go. There's nothing in between us, nothing keeping us apart.

I want to say it to him. I want to tell him I love him. But the feelings are so big, so overwhelming that they get stuck in my throat. I kiss him instead, pouring every emotion into it. All the love I have for him, all the wonder I feel, all the gratitude I have that he came into my life right when we both needed each other.

I tell him with my lips and my tongue, and the message I get back is such a perfect reflection that it brings tears to my eyes.

DONNIE

It's my birthday and Connor's forced me to take the day off work even though I'm already scheduled to be off tomorrow. He says it's the principle of the matter—I'm not allowed to work on my birthday and apparently, *he* has to work tomorrow. He doesn't usually work on Sundays, but there's something about a demanding client and Rick insisting, so I relented, because I can rarely say no to Connor.

He's got a whole day of activities planned, but he won't tell me a single thing. I have to admit, it's kind of nice. I haven't had anyone make such a big deal about my birthday since Roger, and finally celebrating it again feels like another way Connor's bringing me back from the land of merely existing.

He brings me breakfast in bed. His mother's French toast, because it's legitimately very good and I get to cheat on my birthday. He balances it out with a pile of fruit though, so there's that. We sit across from each other on the bed, tray between us.

"You're still not going to tell me what we're doing today?" I ask, taking a sip of coffee.

"Nope." He pops the *p* and looks delighted with himself.

"How am I supposed to know what to wear?"

Connor rolls his eyes. "Something you'd wear to the gym and then something comfortable to change into afterward."

"Like my cycling gear?" I know that's not what he means. It's just fun to tease him.

"I mean, if you want. We're not cycling, though. But I would approve of something tight so I can ogle your ass." He teases right back.

Touché.

We polish off the breakfast and I insist on helping to clean up. Connor lets me but only because it means we'll get out of the house faster. The day is beautiful when we step outside. The mid-summer sun is already high in the sky and it feels like the entire city is out in force. The subway is crowded, which only means that we don't need an excuse to get nice and cozy with each other.

I follow Connor out of the subway and down a familiar street. "There's a climbing gym near here," I say as the dots connect in my brain. "It's owned by some friends of mine."

"Oh, really?" Connor's all innocent and doe-eyed.

"Is that where we're going?"

"I don't know. Maybe?"

"You know about my friends, don't you?" I put my

hands on Connor's sides where he's ticklish and he squirms away before I can get my fingers into him.

"What friends? I don't know anything about any friends."

The lying liar.

Sure enough, both Leon and Tucker are there when we go inside.

"Donnie!" They come out from behind the check-in desk to swallow me up in a group hug. "You came!"

"You knew we were coming?" I ask, peering over their shoulder at Connor who looks smug as hell.

"Yeah, your…" Leon glances at Connor.

"Boyfriend," I say and Connor beams like he's got a spotlight on him.

"… boyfriend called to make sure we'd be here," Leon finishes.

"Do you even remember how to climb, honey?" Tucker asks, which is a good question.

I never considered myself an avid climber, but I popped into the gym regularly enough to have my own climbing shoes. The same climbing shoes that Connor's pulling out of his bag. Where the hell did he find those?

I shake my head at him and he smiles wider.

"I guess we'll see."

Connor does not have his own shoes, so Leon takes him to get him fitted up.

"How've you been?" Tucker asks and for the first time in ages, that question doesn't feel like sandpaper on my soul.

"Good," I say, completely honest. "I'm doing really well."

"You look good." Tucker glances over to Connor and Leon. "Especially with him."

"Yeah." I watch as Connor tries on a pair of shoes. "He's been…" Good doesn't even come close to capturing what Connor's done for me or how he makes me feel when I look at him. It's so incredible it takes my breath away.

Tucker gives me another hug. "Well, whatever he's doing, it's working."

Connor jogs over, shoes and a chalk bag in hand. "I'm ready!"

Tucker points us toward the bouldering section of the gym, then goes back to helping other climbers.

"How did you know?" I ask, pulling Connor close.

"I found the shoes first. Don't laugh, but I thought they were some weird kind of cycling shoes at first."

I definitely laugh, dropping my head onto his shoulder.

"Hey, I said *don't* laugh." He pokes me in the side.

"Okay, okay. How did you figure out they weren't cycling shoes?"

"The internet, duh. And then some Facebook stalking to figure out you used to climb here." His smile turns sheepish. "Is it okay? That I called Leon and Tucker?"

I run my thumb across his brow, across his cheek, and finally, that delicious bottom lip that he's got stuck out in a pout. "Yeah, it's okay. Thank you."

"Good, because I have no clue what to do here, so you'll have to teach me."

I walk him through the colored holds, how to keep his body flush with the wall, how to use his toes to push off. He looks overwhelmed by the time I'm done, eyeing the wall like it's going to collapse on him.

"It's not that bad. Want me to go first?"

He nods, eyes still wide. I pick a V2 route to start with —not too easy, but not hard either. It's been a couple years since I've done this, but the muscle memory should come back to me quickly. The holds are pink and I slowly pull and push myself up the wall until I can tap out at the top. When I climb back down, I'm breathing hard and shaking my arms out.

Connor's eyes are like saucers. "That was so cool."

"Yeah?" I laugh at his enthusiasm.

"Your arms. Your shoulders. Oh my god, your ass."

"Were you just checking me out the whole time?"

"I mean, yeah, isn't that what I'm supposed to do?" he asks. So cheeky.

"Well, it's my turn then." I pat him on the arse for good measure.

We find a nice and easy V0 for him to start with and he flies up the wall like he's made for it. "Can I do it again?" he asks the second his feet touch the thick, cushy mats.

We climb for a couple hours before Connor checks the time and declares that we have to go. We wash the chalk off our hands and change. When I stop to say goodbye to Leon and Tucker, they make me promise to come back again soon.

"Where to now?" I ask when we're back out in the sunshine.

"It's a surprise!" Connor's eyes are shining as he takes my hand and drags me toward the subway.

The surprise takes us to Prospect Park and a group of strangers mingling around a lamppost.

"Wait here." Connor leaves me to check in with the organizer.

My eyes track Connor as he comes toward me. He's so gorgeous with the sun glinting off his hair and his smile makes my heart sing. I take his hand and pull him to me. I still have no idea why we're in the park, but it doesn't matter, as long as I have Connor by my side.

The organizer calls for our attention and then explains what we'll be doing for the afternoon. Foraging for edible plants, then going to a kitchen nearby to cook what we find into a meal.

"Is that okay?" Connor asks softly. "It's like, healthy and stuff."

I plant a big fat kiss on Connor's lips. God, I love this boy so much.

The thought ripples through me and settles deep in my soul. Yes, I do love Connor. With my whole heart. There's no point in denying it anymore, no point in second-guessing myself. I think I may have loved him since that first night at Mars when he wouldn't let go of me in the staff break room. I definitely loved him after he nursed me back to health.

The idea of loving someone else after Roger, of opening myself up again… it's terrifying. What if I lose him too? Does this mean I love Roger less? But it's not about the fear, I realize. It's about the potential of something beautiful and what Connor and I have growing between us is nothing short of dazzling.

"It's perfect."

A tiny bit of pink highlights Connor's cheeks and I argue myself down from taking him home right this minute. As it is, I don't catch much of what our tour guide says. I'm too preoccupied with watching Connor as he roots through the foliage. He's adorable as he compares pictures on his phone to the plants growing out of the ground.

We're being led out of the park to the kitchen when Connor suddenly ducks behind me.

"What is it?"

"Nothing. Keep going." Connor keeps his head down and urges me to walk faster.

I scan the area around us but I don't see anyone I recognize. "Connor? What's going on?"

"Nothing! It's just…" He peeks around my shoulder and I follow his line of sight to a group of people throwing a frisbee around on the grass. "Miles and Wyatt are over there. That's… the friends I used to hang out with."

My arm wraps around him automatically, keeping him behind me like those monsters are going to storm over here and hurt him somehow. I recognize Miles now. He's all wrapped up in another guy and they're laughing like they're having the time of their lives. Well, good for them. Because so are we.

I maneuver us toward the other side of the group we're with so there's no chance of Connor being spotted. "You okay?"

Connor's not smiling the way he was a minute ago, but he doesn't look upset either. Still, they've stolen his sunshine away and that's not okay with me. "Yeah, I'm okay. I don't care anymore. I just don't wanna have to talk to them."

That's more than fair. I wouldn't want him talking to them either. "What about the other people? You said they were your friends?" He hasn't talked about any of them before and I've never thought too much about it.

Connor shrugs and scrunches up his face. "Yeah, but

they're more Miles's friends than mine. Anyway, I don't really miss any of them." He smiles at me and I search for any tension in his expression. I don't find any.

It doesn't sit well with me though. Connor ended up with me that fateful night because he didn't have anywhere else to go, no other friends he felt comfortable enough calling up. If there's anything I've learned in the last several years, anything that Connor's reminded me of, it's that having a community is important. And a community of just me isn't enough, even if I do want to keep Connor all to myself.

I file the thought away for later as we arrive at a stainless-steel teaching kitchen and are given matching aprons. Connor insists on photos—for his office, he says—and so I obediently pose for as many as he wants.

By the time we get home, I'm desperate to strip Connor down and tumble into bed. I push him up against the wall the second the front door is closed and Connor groans into my mouth. He tastes like the creamy mushroom sauce we made with way too much butter. I chase every last drop of it through his mouth.

"Happy birthday, Donnie," he says when I finally let us up for air.

I stare into his eyes, feeling like my heart is bursting, feeling like I'm so full of joy I'm going to drown in it. "I love you."

Connor blinks, then gasps. He looks stunned. "Really?"

I chuckle, because of course that's how he reacts. "Yeah, really. I really, really love you."

His bottom lip comes out and his eyes grow watery with tears. "I love you too."

I know he does but hearing it does something to me. It changes me.

When he slides into my body later, I can't hold back the tears of joy. He fits himself physically inside my body, just like he's fit himself spiritually inside my heart. Perfectly, he fits perfectly.

"I love you. I love you," I whisper to him.

He kisses away my tears and whispers back, "I love you. I love you."

We make love all night, dragging it out until we're both desperate for release. When we finally come, it feels like we're being torn to pieces. I give a piece of myself to him, and he gives a piece of himself to me.

DONNIE

"You met his parents?" Phyllis leans in close, eyes bright with curiosity. "What are they like?"

Since Connor's working today, I agreed to let Phyllis and Leonard take me out for lunch. None of that thick, cloying foreboding this time though. Just joy and comfort at being able to spend time with two people who are important to me.

"They're…" How to describe Kathleen and Harold? "Nice?"

Phyllis rolls her eyes. "That's it? You spend an entire weekend with them and all you come away with is 'nice'?"

I chuckle and shoot a pleading look at Leonard. He sips his wine, like he didn't hear Phyllis's question. He's no help.

"What do you want me to say? They're nice people. They have a lot of friends. They might be a little hard on Connor sometimes."

"Hard? In what way?" Phyllis narrows her eyes, like she's not sure if she approves.

"It's not like that," I say, trying to reassure her, even though my heart warms at how protective Phyllis is over someone she hasn't even met yet.

Leonard's over there doing a piss poor job of holding back his laughter.

"They want the best for him and sometimes, you know, it gets to be too much."

"Hmm." Phyllis makes a show of thinking about what I said. "I suppose I can understand that. And how is Connor's film project going?"

It's been like this all lunch. Connor, Connor, Connor. I'm going to have to introduce them soon so Phyllis can send her questions directly to the source.

"Good, I think. He's met a few people who want to help him make it." I conveniently leave out the X-rated way Sebastian got his start in filmmaking.

"That's lovely. I can't wait to watch it when it's ready."

"I'll let him know." I just hope Sebastian doesn't talk him into including too many naked men in that haunted house.

After lunch, I swing by the cemetery to pay Roger a short visit. No risk of getting caught in the rain this time. The sky is blue and there isn't a single cloud in sight. It doesn't hurt the way it used to. I don't feel like I'm being torn out of my body. There's a sadness that things didn't turn out the way Roger and I had envisioned for ourselves. But also, a joy that we had the time that we had.

"Connor took me climbing yesterday," I say to Roger's headstone. "To Leon and Tucker's gym. I haven't been since, you know. They're doing well. The gym is thriving.

They made me promise to go back more often and Connor had a really good time, so I think we will."

The sun shines down on me, warming my back like it's giving me a hug.

"We went foraging after. Yeah, you heard me. Foraging for mushrooms and plants and stuff. In the middle of Prospect Park. Can you believe it? All part of my healthy eating thing, according to Connor. It was fun though. Not something I ever thought I'd do."

There are birds chirping in the distance.

"I saw your Mom and Dad for lunch. I'm going to bring Connor out to their house soon. Maybe next month. They really want to meet him."

I put my hand on Roger's headstone. It's warm from sitting under the sun all day and I let that warmth seep into me as well.

CONNOR

I peer out of the frosted glass window of our front door, then check my watch again. Where the hell is Donnie? Phyllis called me more than an hour ago saying they were leaving the restaurant and it should've only taken Donnie forty-ish minutes to get home.

Behind me, a houseful of people have already cracked open the booze, so he better get here before the party really gets started.

My phone buzzes in my hand. It's Phyllis again.

"Hello?"

"Still no sign of him?"

"No, and I don't want to message him and accidentally tip him off."

She sighs into the phone. "Maybe he went to run errands or something."

Who the hell runs errands when they've got a surprise party waiting for them at home? Argh.

A deep voice speaks in the background. "Leonard's asking if you'd like us to come in. We're parked down the street."

"Yes, you might as well. No point sitting in the car if we don't know how much longer he'll be."

"Okay, we'll be right there."

An older couple with matching heads of white hair come up the steps a few minutes later and I fling the door open for them. Phyllis immediately engulfs me in a hug so crushing that Mom would've approved.

"Oh my! Look at you!" She squeezes my arms a few times like she's assessing a piece of meat. "Donnie didn't mention how big and burly you are!"

"Um, thank you?"

"Come on, Phyllis, let's not block the entrance." Leonard shakes my hand quickly and escorts his wife inside.

I've spoken to them a few times over the past weeks. When I told them about my plan, they jumped at the chance to lure Donnie out of the house.

I "left for work" this morning and waited for the coast to clear before sneaking back in. Sawyer and Sebastian both came over early to help clear out the backyard and get all the food and drinks set up. Then all of Donnie's old friends—including Leon and Tucker—came pouring in. Any doubts I might've had about whether this party is a good idea were eradicated as one after another said how much they missed Donnie and how excited they were to be at his birthday party again.

A movement through the window catches my eye and I yelp in excitement. I run into the kitchen where everyone is mingling.

"He's coming! He's coming! Everyone hide!" I wave my arms frantically, only to realize there isn't really anywhere to hide in the open-plan kitchen. They all look around at each other, then back at me. "Uh… never mind. Just, shh!"

The front door cracks open and then closes again with a rattle. Donnie's footsteps sound in the hallway, then stop. Silence. Nothing.

I hold my breath. *Come to the kitchen, Donnie.* Why isn't he coming to the kitchen? It's the first thing we do when we get home.

Someone snickers behind me and I throw a glare over my shoulder. Footsteps again, very faint, like Donnie's creeping down the hall. Then he pokes his head around the corner.

"Surprise!"

He jumps and almost hits the ceiling. "Jesus fucking Christ!"

The look on his face is totally worth every minute it took to plan this party. It's absolutely priceless. Donnie sags against the wall, hand on his chest.

"Oh my god, are you okay?" I ask, rushing up to him. "You're not going to have a heart attack, are you?"

He glares at me but he's smiling. "No, but not for lack of trying."

I giggle. I can't help it. This has been so much fun.

"Stop hogging him already!" Leon nudges me aside and drags Donnie into a circle of friends.

I drift back and let them take him. The house is filled with laughter ringing out above the music. Guests spill out of the kitchen onto the back patio and down into the backyard. It's really nice to see the space being used like this, packed with people who love Donnie. This is what it was designed for, I realize. For parties, for people to come together and celebrate each other.

It's sat empty for too long, but not anymore. Not if I have anything to say about it. It's going to be the party house again—every birthday, every promotion, every new relationship, or new child. We're going to fill it with people who are important to us.

I meet Donnie's gaze through the crowd and we exchange a smile. My heart expands with so much happiness that it's a little difficult to breathe. I want to jump up and down. I want to race to the rooftop, throw my arms wide and just laugh. I want to drag Donnie to our bedroom and lock the door. The guests can take care of themselves.

DONNIE

"I love you," I say, cornering Connor in the living room, away from the party. I love the way the words roll off my tongue. I love the way Connor's eyes light up and his cheeks turn pink and his lips curl into a shy smile. I'm never going to tire of saying it to him, I just know it.

"I love you too." Connor kisses me sweetly. "Happy birthday."

I should've known Connor was planning something

with the whole "take the extra day off work" and the "Rick's making me come in on a Sunday." I definitely should've clued in when Phyllis called to invite me to lunch, like she knew I was going to be free.

"I can't believe you managed to track down all these people."

"It took a good amount of snooping," Connor admits, with a self-satisfied smile that he entirely deserves. "Want your birthday present now?"

"Birthday present? This isn't enough?"

Connor tugs me toward the stairs and up to our bedroom. He sits me down on the armchair and disappears into the walk-in closet. He comes out holding a thick envelope.

"This is for you," he says, kneeling down in front of me.

I open the envelope and pull out a cute homemade booklet. *The Complete History of Cycling Filmography*. Inside is page after page of movies about cycling, some documentaries, some silly comedies. I've heard of a few of them and even recognize some of the athletes. But most of the films are completely foreign to me.

"What's this?" I ask.

"It's what we're going to watch for the next few weeks. Or months… I didn't realize how many cycling movies there are." Connor looks sheepish. "Is it too corny? We don't have to if you don't want to."

"Are you kidding?" I pull him in between my knees and kiss him until we're both breathless. "It's fabulous. And so much more fun than watching horror movies."

Connor grins against my mouth. "I figured if I was

going to make you watch films all the time, the least I could do was find ones you'd be interested in."

"I love it," I say between kisses. "I love you."

"I love you too." Connor sighs. "We might have to send Miles and Wyatt a thank you note."

"Why the hell would we have to do that?"

"If it wasn't for them, I would've never been at Mars that night."

"And I would never have brought you home."

"So, in a way, I guess we owe them?"

I scoff. "I don't know if I'd go that far."

"Hmm, I guess you're right. I would've worked up the nerve to talk to Donnie, The Spin Instructor, at some point."

"And I would have noticed the guy in the back corner who smiles like the sun."

Connor shows me that smile again and I melt into his arms.

"I love you, darling."

"I love you too."

EPILOGUE

CONNOR

"I still can't believe you have a full-on theater in your house," Sebastian says as I flick the lights back on. "I'm never reviewing footage on a laptop screen ever again."

"I wish I could take credit for it, but he already had it when I moved in." To *our* house. Not just Donnie's anymore. I get such a thrill out of being able to say that, of hearing other people call it that.

"It just means that you and Donnie were meant to be." Sebastian closes his laptop and slips it back into his bag.

We've been reviewing footage we shot the day before, flagging which takes and which angles we want to use in the film he's helping me produce. It's not fancy, just a short about two guys who meet at a gym and fall in love. The haunted house idea is still in the works—we're scheduled to scout some locations next week.

Sebastian and his boyfriend, Christian, offered to play the main characters of the gym short in exchange for a cut of the proceeds when the film sells. Sebastian's adamant that it will. Me? I'm not as certain, but he's the expert I guess. He's already got a dozen different distribution ideas and it doesn't hurt that Sebastian and Christian have a rabid fan base.

Yeah, that's where I've seen them together before —porn.

Beau and Gavin were kind enough to let us use Mars as a set and we hired a few gym members as background actors. Donnie pitched in some funds to cover the costs. Phyllis and Leonard have too. And after Donnie kept talking up the project with Mom and Dad, they decided they didn't want to be left out.

Figures—they never listen to me, but one word from Donnie and they're all over it. I joke. I was floored by how much they sent over.

"You headed over to Mars?" Sebastian asks as we climb the stairs.

"Yeah, I want to catch Donnie's class this evening. You?"

Sebastian shakes his head. "I went for a run this morning, so no class for me. But I'll go with you to Mars. Christian should be finished by the time we get there."

"Cool. Gimme a minute to grab my stuff." I leave Sebastian in the hall while I run upstairs to drop my computer off in my office.

It's still surreal, thinking of this as mine. I've kept Roger's big desk and his leather executive chair. I swapped out the corkboard for a wall-mounted TV though, for viewing footage. A picture of me and Donnie from the foraging afternoon is framed and sitting on the bookshelf, smiling at me. I love this place. I love Donnie. And you know what, I've never met Roger, but I kind of love him too. He'll always be a part of Donnie's story, so he'll always be a part of mine.

My gym bag is already packed in the bedroom and I grab it before rushing down the stairs to Sebastian again. "Ready!"

Sawyer's at the front desk when we get there, obviously trying not to shout into his phone. "Preston, when was the last time you ate? No, you can't go all day without eating. I don't care how much work you have. That's it. I'm ordering food to the apartment. It better be gone by the time I get home or you're going to be in so much trouble."

I shoot a look at Sebastian. "What's up with that?"

Sebastian winces. "Sawyer's best friend-slash-room-mate. They're a little co-dependent, if you ask me."

A lot co-dependent if Sawyer's keeping track of his friend's eating schedule. But then, Donnie sometimes has to do that with me, so I guess I'm one to talk.

"Sorry, guys." Sawyer ends his call with a shake of his head. "He's working on his dissertation and thinks he can live off of data and citations. I can't tell you how many times I've found him zonked out, face smushed into the keyboard."

"Poor guy." I try to commiserate.

"At least he's got you," Sebastian adds.

"Yeah, tell him that." Sawyer rolls his eyes. "Anyway, we're still on for trivia tomorrow, right?"

The three of us have started going to trivia a couple times a month. I wasn't sure about it at first, since I'm terrible at it. But Donnie really encouraged me to go, so now it's kind of a thing. Sebastian and I both agree, then leave Sawyer to his food delivery app.

We find Christian in the staff locker room, though it'd be more accurately called the staff and boyfriends locker room.

"Hey, babe." Sebastian greets Christian with a camera-worthy kiss.

I busy myself with changing into my gym clothes. Donnie must already be in the spin room, getting fawned over by all his fans. I wave goodbye to Sebastian and Christian and hurry out to find my own boyfriend.

The second I step into the room, his admirers scatter, leaving me with a clear path to Donnie.

"You've trained them well," I say quietly, as he welcomes me into his arms.

"They know I belong to you."

Hell yeah, they do. I kiss him like I haven't seen him in days, just to make sure everyone gets the message. Donnie's mine. Back off.

"Saved your bike for you." Donnie nods at the bike right in front of his. There's a towel slung over the handlebars and I smile as I climb on.

Donnie starts the music and everyone's blood starts pumping. We lean over our bikes and pedal. Donnie's on fire tonight. He's in his element. I crank it when he tells me to, I climb when he pops out of his seat. No matter what happens, no matter what life throws at us, I know one thing for certain. We will always ride together.

———

BONUS SCENE

My hands are stuffed under my thighs so I don't crush the bouquet of flowers in my lap. I'm nervous. Like, a lot. Like, way more than I thought I would be. I wasn't even this nervous when I randomly called up Phyllis and Leonard to invite them to Donnie's birthday party. I wasn't this nervous when Phyllis cornered me at the party and started peppering me with questions.

But visiting Roger's grave is completely freaking me out.

It's not like there's going to be anyone else there to like… judge me or whatever. Except it kind of feels like there is.

I owe so much to this man I've never met. He's given me this beautiful life, an amazing house, a loving boyfriend—I wouldn't have any of it if it wasn't for Roger and the tragedy of his death.

So… it's kinda weird to be like, "thanks for not being here anymore"?

Maybe that's why I'm nervous. A visit to a headstone and a bouquet of flowers is poor recompense, all things considered.

Donnie pulls over at some random spot on the one-lane road that winds through the cemetery. He turns the engine off and looks at me.

"Are you all right, darling?"

To read the rest of the bonus scene, sign up for Linden Bell's Very Important Reader newsletter here: bit.ly/ rippedbonus.

———

STACKED

Do you like best friends to lovers, gay-awakening, nerd/jock romances? Find out just how co-dependent Sawyer and Preston are in the next Mars Fitness book, *STACKED*, bit.ly/stackedbm.

THANK YOU

I am firmly in the nerd camp of the nerd/jock dynamic, but I do enjoy the occasional spin class every now and then. Especially at the gym by my house where the spin instructor has a delicious British accent. ;)

If you've enjoyed *RIPPED*, please consider recommending it to your friends. Leave a review for *RIPPED* on social media, your own blog, Amazon, or Goodreads so other MM romance lovers can get to know Donnie and Connor too.

If you would like to stay up to date on future Linden Bell books, join the Very Important Reader mailing list here: bit.ly/VIRlist.

You can also follow me on:
Facebook - facebook.com/authorlindenbell
Instagram - instagram.com/authorlindenbell
Amazon - amazon.com/author/lindenbell
Goodreads - goodreads.com/authorlindenbell
Bookbub - bookbub.com/authors/linden-bell

ABOUT LINDEN BELL

Linden Bell writes romances that heat you up and make you smile. She's a lifelong fan of the happily ever after, and has recently admitted to being a Trekkie.

- facebook.com/authorlindenbell
- instagram.com/authorlindenbell
- amazon.com/author/lindenbell
- goodreads.com/authorlindenbell
- bookbub.com/authors/linden-bell

ALSO BY LINDEN BELL

Mars Fitness Series

Where the jocks of Mars Fitness meet the nerds of their dreams.

The Camboy Network Series

When sex on camera turns into love behind the scenes.